JED COPE

# Do You Remember

This book was professionally typeset on Reedsy.
Find out more at reedsy.com

*To my Grandparents.*

# 1

The evening had been, as they sometimes say, a resounding success.

And then she hit him.

A rare foray out for a meal. Time away from busy routines.

James had planned it meticulously and when the day had come, he was pleased to see that everything seemed to fall into place. It were as though the universe wanted this for him. This evening was a gift to him for all his hard work and perseverance. James deserved this time out. Melissa deserved this evening. They both deserved it and so the universe granted this small wish.

All the same, James was nervous and on edge and he felt guilty at taking something away from their evening with his burdensome worry. Melissa didn't say anything, she didn't draw attention to his foot tapping away under the table or his darting eyes. Instead, she reached a hand across their table, carefully avoiding the wine glass and salt cellar and she gave his hand a squeeze. He looked at his wife's face for what felt like the first time in a long while and his heart nearly broke in two as she mouthed two simple words; thank you.

James managed a smile and squeezed her hand back. He fought back tears that he didn't know were there, despite feeling them just below the surface for such a long time. He was exhausted. He'd been run so ragged that he no longer knew which way was up.

They should have done this before now. They should have done more of this. Instead they'd gotten on with their lives and been too busy living, only to miss out on the very lives they were living. Or, more importantly, the life they had vowed to share together through thick and thin, until death ended their solemn and love bound contract.

The waiter had chosen that moment to arrive at their table. James thought that this was probably just as well, it had given him something else to focus on and allowed him to compose himself.

The waiter was a man of certain years. His hair greying at the temples and the lines of his face marking at least six decades of life. James wondered whether he was the owner or co-owner of Albertine's. The place had the look and feel of a local, family run restaurant and it was good to have someone wait on the table who wasn't still at school. There was a time and a place for chains and franchises, but that was when there was a lack of time and little room for forethought. The homogenous offering of a *fun* pizza chain was all well and good when you were eating on the hoof and didn't care much for ambience and relaxation. James thought that those days were well behind him and that thought made him feel older than his thirty eight years.

"Would you care to look at the wine and drinks menu?" the waiter said, smiling at Melissa and then at James.

James liked him for that. He'd been subjected to too many interactions where he was focused upon and Melissa was relegated to an appendage, the assumption being that James was the boss and he would decide upon the wine, or the car or whatever it was that the man before them was attempting to sell them.

"Just water, please" James said this automatically and did not fail to spot the flicker of a scowl cross Melissa's face. He quickly relented, "while we look at the drinks menu and decide on another drink," he explained, reaching for the menu the waiter had walked over with.

The waiter smiled, "sparkling or still?" he enquired.

James nodded to Melissa, deferring to her judgement.

"Let's push the boat out," she winked at James, "sparkling, please."

"Very good," smiled the waiter.

He handed the bound menus to first Melissa and then James, "the specials are on the board," and he pointed to the wall behind James, before leaving them to it.

James tried to crane his neck to see what the specials were, Melissa laughed then took pity on him and read them out. James loved the sound of her laughter, this evening was worth it if only for that brief moment. He watched her as she read the specials out to him. The woman he had fallen in love with and married. It wasn't often that he took stock and truly looked at her. No, that wasn't strictly true. He often watched her as she slept. Free of any worries, she looked serene and he always smiled as he gazed upon her. Laughing, sleeping, those moments where life did not weigh heavily upon her. He loved those moments and he loved the woman who took centre stage in those moments.

Melissa gave him a quizzical frown as she finished reading and saw the way he was looking at her.

James shrugged by way of reply and opened his menu, suddenly embarrassed at being caught scrutinising her. He was innocent, but still he felt his cheeks burn, so he stared at the starters until he felt able to speak.

"Shall we go straight into the mains?" he ventured.

"And see if we have room for dessert?" countered Melissa.

He nodded and smiled and turned to the desserts to see if there was anything on the menu that was worth planning for. And of course there was tiramisu, one of James' go to desserts. There was also a Biscoff cheesecake that was a likely contender. Yes,

4

there were desserts that were worthy of their skipping starters.

He turned back to the mains and found that he was skipping hurriedly through them. James was usually a fastidious studier of the menu, he'd peruse the starters then read carefully through each and every main to fully appreciate the entire dish and how well it would suit his tastes. Tastes that shifted and changed sufficiently that should the menu not change, James could enjoy something different on a series of visits to the restaurant in any case.

James knew why he was speeding through the menu. He wanted everything to be right. He wanted a seamless evening. He didn't want the waiter to do that all too common thing where he would return to the table far too soon and then James would have to ask for another couple of minutes, only for the waiter to leave them seemingly stranded and abandoned. He disliked that limbo and the ensuing frustration as he tried to catch someone's eye and began considering how it was that he'd get their order in. An order that would now be queued behind several large groups of diners thus leading to a long wait for their food.

He was trying his best, but he felt under pressure. He was under the clock and he knew it.

"Steak!" he exclaimed a little too loudly as he closed his menu and switched to the drinks menu.

Melissa jumped. He'd startled her. Not good.

"Which one?" she asked.

"The Albertine," he said, already looking forward to the fillet steak sat upon a large ciabatta crouton and accompanied by pate. The red wine gravy and accompanying vegetables sounded spot on and he really fancied a steak, only this was a bit more fancy than the usual steak and chips.

Melissa smiled, "I think I'll have the pork Milanese with spaghetti."

James nodded with appreciation, "that was my second choice."

They both knew what that meant. James liked to order something different to the other diners when they went out. His rationale being that if they all ordered the same then they may as well eat at home. The variety of dishes was part of the experience as far as James was concerned. He liked to see the food and feast his eyes upon the other diners dishes and compare notes on just how good the food itself was. In this case, Melissa and James would try a little of each other's dishes, Melissa reluctantly accepting food from James' fork despite her dislike of being fed by someone else.

He grabbed the drinks menu, "what do you fancy?" he asked his wife.

"You know what I fancy," she winked at him.

He raised an eyebrow in faux disapproval.

6

Melissa smiled and shook her head at him, "I'll have a small merlot," she said.

James was about to say something when the waiter returned, asking whether they had decided. They had and they relayed their food and drink order to him as he noted it on the small pad that all waiting staff sport if they haven't joined the age of tablets and connectivity of all things.

Melissa asked for her merlot as James looked on, she didn't notice the look he gave her, or if she did, she ignored it.

"I'll have a bottle of Peroni," James added. One small drink couldn't hurt, could it?

The meal went without incident. The main courses were excellent and just exactly what Melissa and James had wanted, and they had a little room for dessert. They decided to be good and shared a tiramisu, the size of which was easily enough for two anyway.

As the waiter cleared their shared dessert plate away he asked if they would like a little something to round off with.

"No thanks, just the bill," answered James.

Melissa gave him a disapproving look as the waiter went off to prepare the bill, "that's not like you?"

"How do you mean?" asked James knowing full well what Melissa was getting at.

"You always have a drink at the end of a meal. Especially a meal like this. Why haven't you had a grappa or at least a whisky?"

James shrugged, "I didn't feel like it, besides, I'm driving."

"I'm not," said Melissa pointedly.

James reached across the table and took her hand, "I just want to go home, we can have a drink when we get back, can't we?"

It was Melissa's turn to shrug, she wasn't happy with the James had controlled the ending of their meal.

The of it truth was that James didn't want to push his luck. They had made it through two courses and everything had been fine. The problem was that with the passing of every second, there was the chance of something going wrong and James couldn't countenance that. He wanted to close the door on this evening, take a breath and count this as a success. A victory of sorts. He wanted everything to be OK, even if it was only for this little while.

# 2

The evening had been a resounding success.

And then she hit him.

Everything had been going so well, they'd made it all the way through the meal and the drive home. The drive home was the part that James was most nervous about, he'd had a building anxiety over what might happen in the car, but needn't have worried about that bit. If anything, he'd relaxed and let down his guard, he'd even found he was thinking that everything was going to be alright. It's OK, everything is OK, he had thought to himself as they reached the back stretch of their journey home.

He'd walked up the path to the front door, unlocked it and let Melissa into the house. He took a moment to watch her step over the threshold. She had dressed for the occasion and was wearing a dress and heels. James liked what heels did to the shape of her legs. He was a lucky man, beauty and brains and a kindness that had melted him from the outset. They'd got along like the proverbial house on fire, not that he'd ever got that phrase, the way they had gelled was a little less violent than that. They fit together uncannily and they laughed and they shared a comfortable space that felt more like home than anything James had felt before.

"Oh, I've left my bag in the car!" Melissa cried as James raised his leading foot to enter the house.

She stood there, slightly canted to one side, having kicked off one of her heels, but still wearing the other. She looked like a little girl lost at the oversight of her handbag.

"I'll get it," James smiled reassuringly and turned back to the car. He could hear his heart beat, blood had rushed to his head and he felt slightly dizzy. No, please no, he thought to himself as he walked towards the car, picking his step up to get this over and done with and get back to the house as quickly as he possibly could.

The car was ticking under the bonnet as it cooled. He pressed the fob that had never left his hand, as it also held the front door key. The indicators lit the garden for a few brief seconds and the locks clicked open. James opened the passenger door and the interior of the car was illuminated. He looked on the seat and in the footwell and for good measure he opened the rear door to check the seats and footwells there.

Nothing.

He had known there would be no sign of the bag and now he thought about it, he realised that he'd seen the bag hanging from Melissa's shoulder. He was kicking himself as he returned to the house. Knew why he'd not registered the bag that Melissa was carrying, it was because he dared hope. He'd wanted to believe. He wanted the night to carry on without even the slightest of hitches.

Was that too much to ask?

Thus distracted with his own thoughts, he'd stepped into the house and straight into a completely different situation than the one he'd left only moments before.

"No sign of the..." he'd begun.

Melissa had had her back to him, still wearing the one, heeled shoe. He'd seen her stiffen at the sound of his voice. He'd startled her, and the shock of his sudden return had flipped a switch inside her.

"Who the fuck are you!?" she snarled as she turned to face James.

James reeled at the sudden, unprecedented change in his wife. He did his best to stammer a reply through his shock, "it's me... James... I..."

She stomped towards him, the imbalance of her one shod foot rendering her movement comical. James was not laughing however. Less so as she raised her hand revealing the other shoe, the heel pointing outwards.

"Get out of my fucking house!" she roared before hitting him on the side of his head with her shoe.

There was a violent explosion of pain in James' head as the shoe struck him with considerable force. He went down on one knee at the shock of the sudden violence, his arms automatically raised and seeking to protect his vulnerable head as Melissa struck him again and again and again.

James thought that he'd begged her to stop. That he'd said please, no, stop. But as he lay slumped and bleeding, he'd cried. He'd closed his eyes and cried, only registering Melissa's absence once his tears subsided. He'd never be sure exactly what had happened, only that his wife of seven years had attacked him and that it had hurt. The physical pain was only a small part of that hurt.

With great difficulty he found his feet. Bracing himself against the wall and sliding back upright.

"Melissa?" he breathed the word, feeling a sense of dread as he did.

James eyed the open front door and felt bile rising in his stomach at the prospect of Melissa leaving the house and fleeing God knew where. Then he heard sounds in the living room. Laughter of all things. He shuffled tentatively to the living room door, which was open just a crack, ghostly light moved within. He gently pushed the door open to find Melissa sitting slumped forwards, watching the TV intently. She was still wearing just the one shoe and her handbag lay on the seat next to her.

Spotting movement, she looked up and smiled, "hello love, where have you been?" she turned her head back to the TV and after a few seconds of intent viewing, she laughed again. It wasn't the girlish laughter James had marvelled at at the restaurant, this was an alien braying that chilled James to the bone. That laughter was not his wife's laughter. This, was not the woman James had married.

Safe in the knowledge that his wife was in the house, he left the living room and shut and bolted the front door, then he walked to the cloakroom, leaning on the sink to look in the mirror and inspect the damage. It was a good job the heel on Melissa's shoe was wide. Even so, she'd broken the fragile skin on his temple. He winced as he washed away the blood. There were livid red marks on his face and he'd have a shiner in the morning.

James stifled a sob. They were both young. This was not supposed to be their life! Melissa had only turned thirty five last month. This wasn't supposed to happen. This sort of thing happened to other people and those other people were *old*.

He fought back the tears as he relived the violence that his wife had exacted upon him, only it wasn't his wife. Her face had been transformed. A snarling hateful thing intent on doing him harm. He did not recognise that face and he did not know the person that had done this to him.

And in that horrible moment, Melissa did not know him. Not in that very moment she didn't. James felt overwhelmed by that thought. A well of sadness so deep it had no end, opened up from underneath him. There was something else though. Fear. He wasn't afraid of his wife, he loved her with all his heart, but of their future he was uncertain, and that uncertainty scared him.

$$* * *$$

James returned to the living room, automatically switching on the light.

Melissa looked up at him, blinking and squinting, her eyes not accustomed to the sudden, bright light he had brought with him into the room.

"What time is it?" her voice was tremulous and timid.

They both noticed at the same time. The synchrony of a couple who had been together and made a habit of sharing their lives together. James watched as Melissa's already shaky composure collapsed.

"Oh no!" she gasped.

He moved quickly and decisively and took her arm, guiding her upwards and away from the sofa, "come on, let's get you upstairs and out of those things," he said gently.

He'd taken charge. He needed to do something, couldn't bear to look at her like this. Not his young, vibrant wife. For her

14

part, she went willingly, meekly even. No, this was not his Melissa. Not right now it wasn't.

He helped her get undressed in the bathroom and helped her to the shower. As she washed herself, he took her sodden clothes to the bathroom and rinsed them under the taps until the water was clear, wringing them of most of the water, he took them downstairs and put them straight into the washing machine.

In the kitchen, he grabbed cleaning materials and ran hot water into a bucket. He sponged the sofa down. It wasn't too bad. He couldn't leave the sofa seat cushions where they were though. They'd never dry. He hesitated. Their absence would be a reminder, and worse still, an admonishment. It couldn't be helped though, he took the two damp cushions to the utility room and left them there to dry.

He emptied the bucket and put the cleaning products away. He leant against the kitchen sink and stared out into the darkness outside. Realised that he was looking at his own haggard reflection and sighed. He listened out for what Melissa was doing upstairs. It was quiet. He couldn't hear the shower. That was good, but he couldn't be sure what she was doing. He had to get upstairs.

He had to get upstairs to check on what his wife was doing. That was a horrible eventuality. He felt like a... what? A controlling bastard? He didn't know. All he did know was that it was wrong. Something was going wrong and he didn't feel like he was in control at all, he felt like a passenger. Helpless and clueless and pathetic. He'd been powerless as his wife had launched into him and it was his inability to do anything, his failure to make this right that hurt all the more.

He was losing his wife and he didn't know what to do about it.

He stepped away from the kitchen and made for the door that would take him out to the stairs and up to their bedroom. Part way across the kitchen he stopped, made a decision. He stooped and opened a cupboard door. He shuffled the contents, the movement gave rise to chimes of glass against glass. He found the bottle he was looking for, straightened up and found a tumbler in the wall cupboard above the still open, lower cupboard and poured a generous measure of Talisker. He put the bottle away and took a sip of the single malt whisky, savouring the flavours and the accompanying heat. He barely noticed the burning sensation as the whisky touched his split lip.

He took the whisky with him as he headed up to his wife and their marital bed. He doubted he'd sleep, so he had plenty of time to savour the drink. He hoped it could be a distraction. Doubted that would be the case.

Melissa was in bed, curled up and still. James hoped that she was asleep. He knew that was a cop out. That what he was wishing for was respite from the uncertainty, but surely wishing that his wife had some much needed peace was not a bad thing?

He carefully placed the tumbler on his bedside table and went into the bathroom. He looked around him, momentarily bewildered. Why was he here? He had no business being here. If he cleaned his teeth, his whisky would taste vile. He laughed. He actually laughed at the absurdity of it all. He was having a senior moment. Well, the received wisdom was that if you couldn't beat them, you had to join them, wasn't it? He shrugged as he turned the light out and returned to the bedroom.

He carefully slipped his clothes off and piled them on a chair. Then he slipped into bed, taking care not to awake his slumbering wife. Melissa turned towards him as he lifted his whisky and took a sip.

"Hey!" she said breezily, "where's mine?!"

James must have given her a look. He hadn't meant to, it was a reaction, not a thought out, telegraphed look. It *just happened.*

Melissa's face fell. She was horrified.

"It happened again, didn't it?" she said quietly.

James nodded grimly. What could he say?

"What happened to your face!?" she gasped.

James winced. He'd not expected this, but he should have. Melissa hadn't done this. Only she had. She wouldn't remember it, because she was a different person then and that person had never met his Melissa. Was oblivious to her existence.

"Oh God, James! I'm so sorry! What did I do?" Melissa's voice was wavering. Close to tears. Close to breaking down.

"It's OK," James said quietly, not knowing what else he could say.

Because it was OK. This Melissa was not capable of hurting James. He knew that. This Melissa did not deserve this. Neither of them deserved this.

"It's not OK, James. We have to do something!" Melissa was staring intently at him now.

"We've spoken about this," James thought he sounded defeated. Resigned.

"I know we have, but it's getting worse!"

"We both knew it would get worse though didn't we?"

Melissa's eyes roamed over James face, searching for something. Maybe an answer. He raised his arm. She considered it, resisted the temptation for a short while, then she curled into the crook of it and sighed deeply.

"I don't even know I've had an... episode, if that's what it is. I... I'm so sorry James," she said quietly into his side.

"It's OK, we'll get through this," James said softly, punctuating his words with more whisky.

18

"How?" asked Melissa sleepily.

James didn't answer. They *just would*. He didn't know how. The *how* of it was something they'd have to work at. They were in this together. Through thick and thin. In sickness and in health. He'd always known that you had to work at the worthwhile stuff in life, that you got out what you put in. Only this felt like surviving now. Finding coping strategies and weathering the storm, until...

James didn't want to think about the until. Instead he focused on the rhythmic breathing of his now sleeping wife as he held her close.

Once he was confident that she was sleeping deeply he grabbed his phone and opened the browser. This was when he did a lot of his research on Melissa's condition and how they could cope with it.

# 3

I t had crept up on the both of them.

Insinuated itself into their lives.

Taken it's time as it grew roots and became a part of their reality.

Melissa's *condition.*

If they were to talk about it, they would find themselves saying that it started gently. Things were forgotten. Objects appeared in bizarre locations without a clue, logic or reason as to how they had appeared there.

This *thing* in their lives used them. It used both of them. Hell, it was clever! It used their denial. It used their refusal to believe that either of them could be fallible. They slept walked into their new life whilst the demon who had chosen to come a calling did its worst and all the time it was laughing at them, because this was all a joke. It had to be didn't it?

So gradual had been the process, that neither Melissa or James could pinpoint it's beginning. After all, the low level stuff was common place. Who hadn't mislaid their car keys or walked into a room and forgotten why it was that they had headed there?

People even remonstrated with themselves as it happened; *I never do this!*

That is the denial. The refusal to see that there might just be a problem.

Eventually, the frequency of mishaps increased.

Melissa would lose her train of thought and she became increasingly frustrated at her inability to find it again. She knew something was going on inside her head. She felt an absence. A crushing absence that held with it an inevitability. This wasn't a mental stumble. There, in front of Melissa was a gaping chasm. She dared not look directly at it, but she knew it was there alright.

James had convinced her to go to the doctors.

That had been a grim time. They had fought, which was not at all surprising. They were both scared and lashed out at the one person they knew they could lash out at. They both knew what they feared, but neither wanted to give voice to it. That would only make it real, and right now, they could pretend that it wasn't, that it was all in their heads.

A tumour would do this wouldn't it? Something growing inside

Melissa's head and increasing pressure on her brain so that it had these strange hiccups. And tumours could be cancerous.

The Big C.

Cancer was the wasp of the medical world. An angry bastard of a thing that was itching to sting and sting again. It was merciless and if it so wished it could hit a person hard from the outset so the doctor told them, "I'm afraid it's stage four." Stage four. Just like that. Cancer could grab you and go full throttle so the first three stages passed you by without so much as a by-your-leave.

Melissa wasn't getting headaches or dizzy spells though. They both consoled themselves with that thought and were relieved when she got a clean bill of health. There was no cancer and there was no tumour.

Melissa's GP told them that *things like this happened.* That the body and mind were part of a whole and this was one way that the body told a person to take stock, reassess and bring some much needed balance to their lives.

"You're probably overdoing it," Dr Derwent looked over her glasses at both of them.

James felt like a naughty schoolboy in the headmistress's office. Guilty as charged. Of course they were overdoing it! That's what you did! Work hard and play hard, only there wasn't all that much time for play. If they eased off and did what Dr Derwent was suggesting. If they stopped putting the hours in.

22

Then their progress would stall. They were making hay while the sun still shone. That's what you did in your twenties and thirties so you had a place in the world and once you carved it out then and only then did you think about changing the pace, but James doubted that you could coast. Coasting had a habit of sending you backwards.

That was what you had to do wasn't it?

Surely that was what everyone else was doing?

Dr Derwent gave James an appraising look and then she took her glasses off. This should have softened her features and made her more open and approachable, it didn't. Somehow it had quite the opposite effect. Dr Derwent was about to level with them.

"I regularly get people in here who have been privileged to get a warning, and I sit here and I tell them to listen to their body. Do you know how many of them listen?"

"I..." began James.

"Not enough," cut in Dr Derwent, "my dearest wish is that I could make people stop and listen and change. If they're lucky, their body gives them yet another chance, only this time it goes for a shock tactic, minor heart attack, that sort of thing."

Dr Derwent shook her head and gave forth of a forced laugh, "and still they mostly don't listen. I see families who have lost someone suddenly and inexplicably, and they cry out for that warning so they could have at least tried to do something about it."

She replaced her glasses on her face and held them there for a moment, "I'm sorry. You don't need to hear that. I just get so sad and frustrated sometimes. You're the first patients I've ever said that to."

She'd grinned at them then. Actually grinned. If James had been asked if he thought Dr Derwent was capable of grinning he'd have given a firm *no way* in response. Dr Derwent was not a grinner. Grins did not belong on her face. He was half right, for Dr Derwent's grin transformed her face so radically and it had to in order to take its place amongst her features, it couldn't work any other way.

"Maybe I should do the speech more often? Who knows, it might just work on one or two people and that can only be a good thing, right?" She cleared her throat, "Look, do what you can do to make life easier on yourselves, OK? That can only be a good thing. I'm not advocating that you quit your jobs and go find yourself in a tent on the other side of the world, just make some adjustments. Proper adjustments that make a difference. Don't burn yourselves out, or worse..."

Burn out.

That made sense.

Mental exhaustion.

They had listened and if anything, they had grabbed a hold of this need for change and balance and really gone with it. When James looked back, he thought maybe they knew even then. That even without a diagnosis and a label they at least had an idea that they had a serious cuckoo in their particular nest.

Melissa quit her job. Only, she didn't quit it as much as change the way she went about it. She decided this was the push she needed and that it was high time that she went out on her own. She was a graphic designer and she had enough of a name and reputation to go freelance. No daily commute and the luxury of picking and choosing her assignments and hours? What wasn't to like?

As with many things in life, especially the big things, the reality of the change wasn't quite like that. Giving up the guaranteed and regular pay cheque and the structure of work, placed additional stress on them both. For a good while, Melissa couldn't pick and choose her work. She struggled to fill her days and as a result she took on work whenever she could. This meant that at times she was flat out and then some, only to have a dry spell which was stressful and more draining than a quiet day in the office as a wage slave.

She got there though and the change seemed to do both of them both the world of good. Everything seemed fine while they were in this busy period.

It wasn't though.

Things were far from fine.

They were both just too busy to see that.

# 4

Whenever James searched for information on Melissa's condition, he always tried to look up something a little different, but didn't really make much progress. Knew that he couldn't get much further. There were hints, tips and coping mechanisms. It was all about managing things. Really it was the same as life. There was never a magic bullet, only pointers as to the work that you really should put in to make a good fist of things.

James had to remind himself of that. That he and Melissa had lives ahead of them and it was about making appropriate and good choices and then putting the work in to make those choices stick.

He found himself reading another article on the dos and don'ts of what you should say to someone with a degenerative brain condition. He no longer searched for miracle cures or anything that would at least stem the flow of Melissa's memories and brain function. There was nothing. James tried to look at it as general wear and tear, some of which you just had to live with, you might replace a hip or a knee, but when your brain wore out, that was it. You just had to make do with what you had.

James read the advice on memories, he read that he should begin with 'I remember', as opposed to leading with 'do you remember', that it was important to gently lead and not put the onus on Melissa. Her short term memory may be slipping, but he had heard a number of times of people with dementia recalling long term memories and enjoying time with those recollections. This was something that he should bear in mind and try to encourage, to take her away from the here and now and travel to times when life was simpler. When life was still good.

In the end, they had given up on the doctors and hospitals. Melissa had after all been given a clean bill of health in the first place. Once the symptoms conspicuously manifested themselves and kept on coming, they both knew the score even before they looked it up.

The first phase of an illness like this was silent. There were no symptoms. The rot set in first and then it crept out and made itself known. They'd also skipped to the important part and looked up the possible outcomes, coming to the conclusion that Melissa probably had ten years of life left to her.

It was anyone's guess how many of those years were going to be *normal,* but after today's performance, James reckoned that they'd passed normal some time back and now they were out in unchartered territory.

His mind wandered and he sighed. They had been talking about having kids. That was the next thing on their notional list. Melissa had raised the subject a few times and James was

28

coming around to it. Time had a habit of getting on with its thing and leaving people behind and they already knew couples who were struggling to get pregnant. Could see the pain those couples carried around with them.

James had spoken often with his friend Craig, he and his girlfriend Ann were *trying.* This meant that they had stopped taking contraception and let nature take its course, only nature hadn't gotten with the program and wasn't playing ball. Craig admitted that they did their odds no favours during that period as the sex was almost non-existent. One or both of them was asleep by the time they had a window of opportunity. This had led to recriminations, or rather the fear of them and making pre-emptive strikes. Along this rocky road, they built up a head of steamy stress that was never going to do them any favours even if they did manage to do the deed. However much they tried to relax and not load the bases, they didn't. Their focus was totally on baby making and the fun, joy and release of the physical act of sex was banished to the good old days before their overriding need to procreate.

Now Ann had a timetable of sorts. She monitored her body and the timing of her ovulation and when the time was right, Craig was required to scramble his fighter and drop his bouncing bomb with absolute precision. Ann's dam still held and now they were at the stage where they wondered which one of them was at fault.

James felt for his friend, they'd been to school together and been oblivious to how easy it was for some of girls in their class to fall pregnant. It was only later when they saw those girls pushing prams that they realised what the weight gain and absences from school were really about. During those heady years of ignorance and gradual awakenings they encountered the concept of unwanted pregnancies. These were a consequence of *doing it,* but not taking the correct precautions. Or taking the correct precautions but something going wrong anyway. They heard horror stories about jonnies splitting. They weren't quite sure how this might happen, and what problems it would cause, but it all sounded horrible and messy and something to be avoided at all costs, so they both came to this particular party later and were grateful for that extra year or two of maturity. Waiting was wise. Waiting saved them riding headlong into a brick wall of adulthood without wearing a crash helmet, let alone leathers.

Plenty of time for that.

That was what their parents and adults repeatedly told them.

Don't rush! There's loads of time!

Only there wasn't. No one told you about the inconspicuous tipping point where plenty of time swung right across to not enough time.

It really didn't help that there were a crowd of older people yelling at Craig and James to put the brakes on, but no one had ever given them a nudge and told them to ease their foot off that middle pedal. Oh, there had been the occasional lone voice. James' granny would cut through the chatter at family dos and ask him when he was going to give her beautiful grandchildren.

## 4

She always picked her moment and her voice carried in a way that stopped all conversation and drew full attention to James. He'd feel the heat in his cheeks even as she began, then all eyes would be on him and there would be a chorus line of aunts and uncles who joined in.

"Yeah James, when are you going to *do the deed*!?"

"Time to make babies, James!"

"Do as your granny says!"

He'd never taken his granny seriously. Besides which, when-ever she'd put in her request he'd not been ready. Mostly because he'd not had a receptacle for baby making in his life, or if in theory this was the case, he or she were not sure whether they were in it for the long haul and so the theoretical possibility of making a baby stayed just that.

Now though?

At least we don't have the prospect of a string of unsuccessful IVF attempts, thought James. He'd seen friends and colleagues go through the process. Hospital and clinic visits, injections, samples, testing and consultations. Huge fees. Personal research and consideration of travel to increase the chances of a successful attempt and full term pregnancy. All the time wondering how the outcome would affect their relationship. Even a successful outcome after all that exhausting and stress-ful work may not be enough to keep the couple together, not after all they'd been through. And if one of them couldn't give the other what they wanted?

Not for James and Melissa, the rollercoaster ride of parenthood. James' granny would never see his grandchildren. But then it really was too late as far as she was concerned now, his dear, eccentric, funny and entertaining granny had passed away the year before. She'd fallen ill and declined, there was a suggestion of dementia, but she had been so scatty and flighty they had never been quite sure whether it was dementia or not. Perhaps it was a mercy that she had gone so quickly. A mercy for her, but not for his grandpa. Once grandpa admitted defeat and realised that he couldn't continue looking after his wife of over sixty years his decline from spritely octogenarian to bed ridden care home occupant was shocking. The twinkle in his eye didn't take time to dim, it was extinguished as soon as he lost his purpose in life. James sat helplessly and watched his hero die. There was nothing any of them could do. They tried. But his grandpa's heart wasn't in it anymore, and they all knew it. This was his time.

Their funerals were within a week of each other.

With what he knew now, James thought back to his grand-parents. He thought it likely that his granny had been ill for quite some time, but his grandpa had managed it all. Kept up appearances and ensured that they stayed together in their home where they belonged. He probably didn't want to bother anyone and cause any fuss, so he became the glue that kept them and their lives together.

How many years did that go on for and how hard did he work

to keep up appearances? James wondered how hard that must have been, but then, his grandpa had had no alternatives, or at least felt that he didn't, and in the final analysis he'd been right, hadn't he? Was it that way, or had his grandpa made it that way over those last years? Invested himself so heavily in his life that once it was taken from him, and his wife of over sixty years had to go into care, he had nothing left to live for?

James felt the tears come. You still had me grandpa, he whispered to himself. He wasn't crying with the frustration of losing his grandpa, even back then he'd understood and respected the old man. He had never seen what had happened as selfish, he saw it for what it was, he couldn't live without his wife. He was crying because he could see so much more of it all now. He was crying because now he was in the same boat and faced with the exact same choices, only he didn't have a brood of kids and grandkids around him.

Did that make it easier though? Fewer people to feel obligations towards.

This was going to be far from easy.

And after? What then? Would he have anything left in the tank?

# 5

"Oh! I've hit a raw nerve have I?!" bawled Simon.

"You're not being fair Simon," James said quietly, refusing to rise to Simon's bait.

James was feeling sick to his stomach. He hadn't thought for one moment that this would be easy, nothing was going to be easy from now on in, but he hadn't expected Simon to behave so badly. Only... he had. He knew that Simon had this side to him, but James was seldom on the receiving end, in fact, he'd never been on the receiving end, unless you counted a couple of drunken arguments where they'd both had one too many and walked away with no memory of the subject matter of their argument, only the certainty that *they were right.* That certainty was cast iron and drummed up a chest puffing fervour the next morning. A passion that would not be quelled. So it was just as well that they gave each other a wide berth and calmed down enough to realise that it couldn't have been all that important if they couldn't remember what they had quarrelled over.

James did recall a drunken argument he'd had with Melissa

when they had been dating and Melissa reminding him in the morning that it had all been over a sachet of mustard at the take away pizza place. James invoked the case of the argument-causing mustard sachet when he thought that perhaps he was being unreasonable, it was a very good example of how unreasonable James was capable of being, especially when under the influence of the alcohol.

Part of the problem was that Simon didn't need to be drunk to get angry and unreasonable, he just needed to get angry and anger was never reasonable and for Simon it was never far from his surface.

Their partnership worked so well because they complimented each other. It wasn't as simple as good cop and bad cop, but there was something of that there. James knew when to reign Simon in and prevent things getting nasty. James would step in and deal with things in a calm and professional manner, but he was very aware that the threat of a snarling and dangerous Simon had been a catalyst for a speedy conclusion to matters and results that went in their favour. For his part, Simon was the engine room, he pushed things through and James went along with most of it, unless he could see trouble ahead. James tempered Simon's temper and kept things largely on the straight and narrow.

Now James was facing the trouble head on and there was no one to pull Simon away from this confrontation.

"Fair? Fair! You make me so angry when you're like this."

"Like what?!" James hissed, barely containing his own anger.

James couldn't help it, he knew it was the wrong thing to push back, potentially incendiary where Simon was concerned, but this was important. This was more than important, it was vital. Simon should know that he would never ask this of him unless it was life and death. They'd put everything into this partnership and that included their trust. They'd backed each other and invested everything into their business.

"This!" barked Simon.

James shook his head, "you're going to have to give me a little more to go on, Simon."

"And there you go!" laughed Simon. It wasn't a good laugh, it was an angry laugh. Simon was building his anger and that was never good, when James looked none the wiser he bit down and carried on, "your sanctimonious therapist act. The role you all too easily took to control me. Only you take the higher ground and talk down to me, you treat me no better than a dog. It seems that James evolved, but poor Simon is still a base animal who needs to be kept on a short leash! Oh! You're fine with setting me on people, but when you've had your fill you can't even bear to be in the same room as me!"

"I..." began James, not even knowing how to defend himself, but knowing any attempt would be futile right now. Part of Simon's MO was to build his own story and own it completely via his anger. Listening wasn't an option when he got like this, or if he did listen, all that accomplished was further material for his own story. Simon was in attack mode and would take no prisoners now. It didn't help that although exaggerated, his words weren't a million miles from the mark. James almost wanted to congratulate him on this feat of self-awareness, he'd never exhibited anything like it in all the years that he had known him. James took a mental step back, if he was thinking like this then they were both on dangerous ground.

"I've seen the way you look at me!" he spoke in a voice loaded with malice, "then you pull *this!*"

*This.*

That was what it boiled down to right now and Simon had a point with *this.* Simon wasn't being fair and he certainly wasn't cutting James any slack, nor taking into account anything other than *this,* but then James hadn't approached the conversation well. How did you approach something like this though? James didn't want to talk about it. Maybe that meant he wasn't dealing with it, only he was taking the time out to deal with it right now, so go figure. The reluctance remained though and it had done him no favours.

What was he supposed to say?

Didn't he have a right to keep things private and retain some dignity?

James supposed there was the stigma of the illness itself. Anything to do with mental health was taboo. You didn't talk about mental illness. People may campaign for awareness, there might be a desire for there to be more understanding, but James had thought long and hard about this. Society had rules. People needed those rules. They needed structure and they needed to know where they were with other people. So yeah, they might not refer to someone who was ill as mental or wrong-in-the-head, but at the very least they were wary. Some of that wary was protection, not protection from the illness itself, but near as damn it because mental illness took a toll and the ripples it caused were difficult to deal with.

If you wanted proof in that particular pudding, look at the way the entire country treated its elders and betters. Only they were no longer better. They were deteriorating and provided a constant reminder of what was awaiting everyone. Weakness and mortality and ultimately death were part of the whole taboo.

*She's dying...*

Is that what James should have led with? Because that was the truth of it wasn't it?

James didn't want to have to answer the natural question, the question everyone asked when news of a terminal verdict was delivered.

*What of?*

There wasn't even a clear cut answer to that one. If James said dementia, he'd be challenged on it. Dementia wasn't a young person's disease. That's why it had to be qualified with the words early onset. Early Onset Dementia, as though Melissa had caught this particular bus at the crack of dawn to beat the rush. Simon would expect an explanation of Melissa's plight and recounting what was likely to happen to her was too much. James didn't want to give it words and why did he have to? If it was cancer he'd only have to say that, maybe add what kind of cancer it was and qualify it as being the full on kind that ate someone from the inside out.

How did that work? If the Big C was eating Melissa's brain right now, then people would understand. That it was the inexplicable deterioration of her mind meant that her illness was viewed through a different lens and somehow it didn't count.

It was in her head.

Even James couldn't take dementia as seriously as cancer because the so called experts didn't know enough about it. Was that a part of the way society hid the elderly? Shipping them off to isolated homes where they may or may not get obligatory and awkward visits? Dementia affected old people who were going to die in any case, so what was the point in spending billions of pounds researching a cure for something that affected people in their twilight years? People who had already outlived their usefulness. After all, we were all going to die and there was a limit to the years that people could live. Tinkering with diseases and conditions that had no overall statistical impact on life expectancy was not high up on anyone's list of priorities.

James' own grandparents had ended up in a care home. Not for long, but the fact remained that his extended family couldn't care for them. Where was the line between couldn't and wouldn't? Anything was possible, wasn't it? But those possibilities had a cost and knock on effects for all involved. People struggled to care for themselves, let alone their kids or their partners.

He knew he was avoiding one of the Big Questions that was looming up ahead of him and that would have to eventually be answered.

What was James going to do when he could no longer care for Melissa?

That day would come. He knew it. However hard he tried and whatever he did, he would need help. *They* would need help. James would have to admit defeat and let people into their home, forever changing it and their lives. Right now, James couldn't face that. It was as much as he could do to take these first, much needed steps. That was how you did it, wasn't it? You got on with the job in hand? He'd admitted he couldn't run a business and also care for his wife, so he was making changes to accommodate these developments in his life, but right now, Simon wasn't playing ball.

Simon wasn't playing ball because James hadn't been straight with him. James was in partial denial and he didn't want to admit to himself that his wife's brain was dying and that she was already a different person than the person he'd met, fallen in love with and married.

Things were not going to plan.

He knew that Melissa would change. He'd expected that. They would grow together. That was life. You were a different person today to the one you were yesterday. Now dementia had come along, Melissa had stopped growing though and James didn't have a bead on who she was going to be. For some reason, he found himself looking back at the time he had been dumped from his first, formative relationship. He and Tracy and met at sweet sixteen and gone steady for years. Taken things easy and gotten to know each other. A lot happens over those sunshine years though, and they were both busy with school and studying and friends, and James also held down two jobs outside school. He'd thought that they were serious and perhaps maybe they were going to be those almost childhood sweethearts that lasted the distance. That was how he saw things and maybe that meant he took the outcome for granted and in taking it for granted, maybe he didn't put the work in that he needed to.

Maybe that was how it was.

He also thought that, should there be a problem, then his friend would say something, because when it came down to it, Tracy was his friend. A special friend. Why wouldn't she say something?

Things don't always go to plan. They don't always follow a person's expectations, and this was how James and Tracy panned out. One day she told him she was seeing someone else. That was when she decided to say something.

The world stopped turning for a moment and James was poleaxed. This was a sucker punch and then some. He felt like a giant teddy bear, fuzzy, woolly and set apart from the world of people, only Tracy had undone his stitching and was pulling his insides out.

James had not seen this coming, but he did see something now. Tracy thought that he knew. Tracy thought that this was an obvious conclusion and his reaction was a complete surprise to her. What he also saw was a different person to the one he'd seen before this moment. It wasn't just that this couldn't be *his* Tracy because his Tracy couldn't and wouldn't do this, it was that she had chosen to embark upon a clandestine project where she became a different person and once she'd succeeded in building this new person, she was always going to jettison James and with him, her old and now superfluous self.

So people changed. That change was natural, and sometimes the changes were painful.

Tracy's change had been painful for James. It didn't help that he was made up of all these conflicting parts including an ego. His ego found dealing with the betrayal really difficult. When James looked back though, he could see that Tracy's change was a common story that played out time and again. Yes, there were better and more pleasant ways to make those changes, but once the initial, painful moment had passed, it was onwards and upwards. If anything, at that stage in their lives, their break up was part of growing up and James had learned a great deal from that time in his life. He might not have put some of it into practice for quite some while after that, but eventually he got that you had to work at things if they were going to endure. That he was a growing and changing person and anyone he shared his life with was too, so he had to think and consider and respect and make darn sure that he talked and some of that talking was talking things out and dealing with them.

Melissa was now changing in a direction that James had never expected or anticipated, and while he continued to face forwards, she was effectively going backwards. Only most of her wasn't. Some of her was going backwards and that part of her would grow while the vibrant forward looking person James knew and loved would diminish. There was no sugar coating that. He had to accept it and alter his perspective so he could live with it and deal with it. Only then would he continue to see the good in the situation and in his wife.

James had to admit that he didn't have a clue and he didn't know what he was doing. No wonder he'd made a complete hash of this difficult exchange with Simon.

Simon was glowering at him. It was his trademark challenge. A stand-off, but a stand-off with Simon taking the higher ground and waiting to pounce on his prey.

"Look I didn't mean to..." began James.

"Leave me in the lurch? Leave us all in the lurch while you take time out to bloody well find yourself! You wishy-washy *twat!*"

James baulked at his friend's words and his tone, but strangely found something positive in his election of swearword. He'd spat the word out as though it were a much worse word, Simon could do that with aplomb so a person was in no doubt as to what he really though, but still he'd made an effort to tone it down.

James wanted to capitulate and to make it all alright, but couldn't find it in himself to do it. He was angry too! Not the same anger that Simon seemed to have an endless supply of. James' anger was laced with resignation and frustration, but he couldn't give in. He couldn't slump or he'd never get up again.

"It's not like that," James said simply.

"Well tell me what it *is* like," Simon demanded, "you at least owe me that if you're going to go soft on me and give up on what we both worked so hard to build. You walk away now and we're both fucked – there's so much more we need to do!"

James looked at his friend. Simon had tempered his tone and he was trying to reason with him, at least he was in his own way. James got how much that had taken. James couldn't. There were no words. He felt this pressure inside him and a well of emotion that had come from nowhere. Filling him and suffocating him from the inside. His eye sight blurred and he felt dizzy, this must be what a panic attack feels like, he thought to himself in a detached and strange sort of way.

He was already walking for the door when words eventually came to him.

## 5

"Melissa's dying."

He wasn't certain whether he said them out loud or not. All he could think of was getting out of there and into the open.

# 6

J ames had never found himself in a pub without an idea as to how he had gotten there. Not stone cold sober anyway. There was a first time for everything, he thought as he ordered himself a pint, pointing at a likely pump and saying "pint," to keep the interaction as simple as possible.

His voice seemed strange to him even as he uttered the single word. He was strange. This was all strange.

He'd never had a panic attack before, if that was what had just occurred. He didn't know what had happened and was that really a surprise when his entire world had been sabotaged from within. How fragile was the construct of a reality that it could be undone in a matter of moments?

This one was a corker though, because James couldn't build from here. He couldn't even rebuild. He had to watch his life deconstructed brick by brick and all he could do was survive.

No, he was going to make the best of it. That was the advice his grandparents would have given him, and that generation bloody well knew what they were talking about.

6

You made the best of it.

House blown up?

You made the best of it.

Nearest and dearest killed?

You made the best of it.

Nazi menace amassing at the borders of your country and invoking Blitzkrieg on your asses?

You made the best of it.

So how dare he indulge in snivelling self-pity, especially when none of this was actually happening to him. OK, it *was* happening to him, because they were in this together, come what may, but he wasn't the one with the broken head. He wasn't the one with the nightmare that had parked inside his mind. Whatever happened, he would be alright. He would survive because that was what he had to do, and he had no right to do anything other than survive. He just wished he could *do* something to take it all away.

He also wished he could be up to all of this.

He *was* panicking, because he didn't know whether he could do this. He wasn't going to run away. He was going to be there every step of the way, but there were other ways that you could run away, there were ways of not being there even when you

47

were physically present. Could he really *be there* for Melissa.

"Like that is it?" said a voice to his right.

He turned his head and looked dumbly at the only other occupant of the bar. A man he had not until then noticed, so caught up was he in his own predicament.

The man at the bar smiled a wry smile and nodded. It *was* like that, "Get the man another pint, John. His first one seems to have evaporated."

James turned his head back and dropped it mechanically towards his now empty glass, unaware as to how it came to be empty, "Thanks", he managed as he tried to catch up with the events around him. He felt better than he had as he left the offices and Simon, but this wasn't normal.

Normal? What the heck was that? You grew up being taught how to be normal, to be what people expected, or at least operate within the confines of normality, and then this. Normal had been taken away from Melissa and so it had been taken away from him too. Nothing would ever be normal again.

"There you go," said John the bar man as he handed a fresh pint to James, "go a bit easier on this one, eh?"

"Heresy!" cried the other bar occupant in mock disapproval, "think about your takings, John!"

John laughed, "always count on you to keep me on the straight and narrow, Sean!"

James laughed in spite of himself. There was something warming and infectious about the light-hearted exchange. The feel of the place was different for there being just the three of them. Intimate somehow, like he was visiting a friend's home and relaxing in their living room. He found that he *was* relaxing as he sat at the bar. He took a slow and more considered drink of his second pint. As he placed it down, he looked at the pump to see what it was he'd ordered. Timothy Taylor's Landlord, it seemed that even while out of it he had an innate sense of taste when it came to beer.

He sat there for a while, lost in his thoughts. Realised he was staring at his reflection in the mirror behind the bar. Wasn't quite sure what he saw anymore. His mood changed, it wasn't that he snapped out of whatever state he had been in, the transition was more gentle than that. He was now open for business and this became self-evident to the other two occupants of the room.

John merely smiled and nodded at James' now empty pint glass.

"Yes please, another," he glanced at his bar mate before adding, "and one for this gentleman here and one for yourself."

"Very kind of you," said John doing the honours.

James noted that he didn't *put the drink away* as it was some-times referred to, the concept being he'd have the drink later, when really he'd take the money instead, no he poured himself a pint of lager and Sean, his bar mate a pint of Guinness.

James assumed that Sean was a bar fly. A man of middle years who spent a good deal of time at the pub. This was a casual and somewhat lazy assumption and were a third punter to have walked into the pub, not a regular mind, they may well make the same assumption about James. Sean though had the demeanour and look of a bar fly. He *belonged*. And he had already demonstrated that casual air and easy wit of a man used to his station at the bar.

Sean raised his glass, "Cheers," he said before quaffing a good third of his drink and bestowing upon his face a considerable white moustache, "Ah!" he added in appreciation of his drink.

James smiled, "I've not been to this pub before."

He realised that he didn't know the name of the pub and quickly scanned around for clues as to what it was called.

"I know," said Sean, "it's the Red Lion," he added.

James gave Sean a closer look, he knew he hadn't just had his mind read, but the man had just read him all the same.
    "You got me there" smiled James.

"Not difficult really," Sean leaned back and made an exaggerated and expansive gesture, "a man bowls into a pub with the sort of thirst on that you had? He's unlikely to attend to such details as the name of the first pub he espies. Just a spot of the old deductive reasoning."

50

"Right old Sherlock, ain't he?" quipped John, the bar man.

James smiled, "He'd give the famous detective a run for his money."

"Doubt that," shrugged Sean.

"So, with a sharp mind like that, what do you do with your days?" asked James, keen to find out a little more about this man at the bar. Sean certainly had something about him.

"Straight in there with the questions that count!" observed Sean, "we'd best watch this one, John!"

James took a drink from his pint, savouring the taste and awaiting an answer from Sean. He noticed Sean had become a little less open, leaning back into the bar and arms brought in towards his body. Sean gave James an appraising look.

"I'm not a fan of the *what's your day job* question. It's a bit crude, really. And how often do people ask that question, only to go nowhere else with it, just a simple and closed response, *oh that's nice.* Bit pointless really. Or rude. Because were I to tell you I were a lion tamer? Well then I'd get twenty questions! But if I tell you I'm an accountant or an actuary, well you'll wish you never asked. Those guys belong in the kitchen at a house party. I think there's better questions to ask a person if you want to know more about them."

"Like what?" asked James.

"I dunno!" grinned Sean, "that's my theory, I haven't actually done the legwork on it!"

"Oh," nodded James.

He got where Sean was coming from, people asked questions out of habit. They'd ask how someone was, but weren't at all interested in the answer. If there was an answer it would often be met with disinterest or discomfort. James thought he might also be breaking the unwritten rules of the pub, or at least this pub, or Sean's personal rules. He'd known people who gave away very little of themselves and it made sense that someone who chose to take themselves away to a bar may well be doing so to avoid interaction with people. The stereotypical husband choosing a night at the pub in favour of the alternative night stuck in front of the TV with his wife. Or maybe there was no one at home to share anything with. If someone at a bar wanted to talk, they would. And when they did, often no one wanted what they were offering anyway.

Life, thought James, was a bundle of perverse contradictions.

Sean leant forwards, taking on a conspiratorial air, "as you asked, I will tell you something, stranger..."

"James," said James.

Sean nodded, "Well James, I'll tell you what I am. I'm a bloody superhero is what I am."

James gave Sean a quizzical look, then turned to see if John was following this. Sean had seemed so together and *stable* until this comment. Was this a joke?

"He's serious," said John in a very serious tone.

Sean continued, "You see, life is a bit of a joke isn't it? Whoever built us was in a mischievous mood at the time and the joke has been on us ever since."

"You're right there," agreed James.

This struck a chord and Sean seemed to sense this. He appraised James, "ah, I see we have an alumni of the School of Hard Knocks, Jonathon. I think this calls for a stiffener."

Sean nodded at the optics and John did the honours. James noticed that the till was left untouched and Sean noticed him noticing this. Sean winked. James thought maybe Sean was the owner of the establishment, but whether this notion would ever be confirmed was another matter.

Sean raised his glass of whisky and James and John did likewise, "to life," he said quietly and reverently before taking a sip.

"And all who sail in her!" added John.

They all raised their glasses to that and had another drink. There followed a companionable silence and James enjoyed a moment in the warm glow of the whisky, tucked away from the world outside.

"Superhero," he said eventually.

"What..." Sean had drifted off into his own thoughts, "ah! Yes!"

He took another drink, then poured the remnants of his whisky into his Guinness before continuing.

"You see, you have to be careful of what you wish for and I am an example of that. Every little boy, and girl for that matter, wants to be a superhero don't they? They want to be special and make a difference. And I am."

Sean waved his hands around his person to point out his amazing difference. James wasn't seeing it.

"Of course, it isn't visible!" protested Sean, noticing James sceptical look, "and I don't wear an outfit under these clothes of mine. Urgh! I really haven't got the figure for it! So let's not be so superficial. Many of the best things cannot be seen. Love for instance."

Sean ticked off a finger as he said this, he then looked at his finger and considered it, or more precisely, considered additional invisible items of wonder. Then he thought better of it.

"Anyway, the power I have is a curse and what makes it worse is that when I tell people of my power there is then no escaping it. It is your typical self-fulfilling prophesy I'm afraid."

Sean gave James a hard look. There was a comical edge to it.

This was a look that James had never had bestowed upon him before.

"You're not running," stated Sean, "he's not a runner, John. Get the man another pint, he'll need it!"

John did the honours, pouring three pints and distributing them accordingly. James noticed that again, the till remained untouched. They all went at the fresh pints. James fleetingly wondered where his previous drinks had gone. They seemed to be taking care of themselves when it came down to the drinking of them.

There descended again a companionable silence, aided and abetted by the drinking of beers.

"So your power?" prompted James.

"He's intent on opening my little Pandora's Box isn't he John?"

John chuckled by way of a response.

"Didn't you know that curiosity killed the cat, James?"

James nodded and smiled.

"Think about that for a moment, we none of us do enough of that, cats have nine lives and yet when they stick their nose in where they shouldn't, they're goners. Yet we carry on blithely. It's a wonder we've lasted as long as we have as a species."

Sean scrutinised James before proceeding, "There's not a snappy name for the power I wield. That's part of the joke really. I'm not super. I don't have the characteristics of a bat and yet walk the night as a man. No, I am not simple. You may have now gleaned that I am many things, but simple is not one of them."

James nodded. Sean could definitely tell a tale and string something out. He just wanted the punchline now.

"I am," said Sean, "a problem. A conundrum. A catalyst for chaos. And the worst of it? There's nothing in it for me! Oh, you may say that that there is a superhero's lot. That with great power comes great responsibility and that is a burden, not a joy. But heroes are revered and their rewards are the tales that are told about their deeds. They stand proud upon a job well done. Yet I have none of that!"

Sean was really getting into this now. His speech was impassioned and driven and James found he was also getting into it. He was invested in it.

"I am, Bring-Out-The-Worst-In-People Man," boomed Sean theatrically.

"You what?" blurted James.

"I told you it wasn't catchy," Sean sounded a little hurt, "we've tried other names, haven't we John?"

"We have," agreed John, who had taken up a glass and a bar

towel and was polishing vigorously.

"We have found no alternative name," said Sean gravely, "I'm sure I am not the only superhero who suffers in this respect."

James found himself actually thinking over super hero names and trying to locate a rubbish one. He shrugged as he came up blank. The best he could do was The Flash. He'd never really got that name. It was at least a bit dated and also ran the gauntlet of being misconstrued as something pretty unbecoming.

"You're not going to be a success in the world of superheroes if you don't have a catchy name. I'm a marketing nightmare," groaned Sean.

"OK, but what do you mean. How does it work?" asked James.

"Don't ask me! Do you know how you work? All I know is that it does."

"It does," confirmed John laconically, still polishing the same glass.

"OK, give me examples," demanded James bullishly.

"I will not," stated Sean, "each manifestation of my powers is personal to the recipient. Although there are areas of commonality and I can put people into groups. Besides, I would not want to lead you, after all, we all have choices and we like to be in control. Or at least we keep hold of the illusion of control don't we?"

"This is bullshit!" James found himself guffawing.

"And so it begins," Sean waved in James' direction.

James came up a little short. Shocked at his own outburst. He wasn't usually like this. Especially not with people he'd only just met. That was a bit off. He looked askance at Sean.

Sean nodded in reply and gave a brief, wry smile.

"I think it is time we took our leave John," said Sean.

John nodded, "Yes indeed. If you could finish up, sir. That would be most appreciated."

James looked from one to the other of the men, feeling affronted and out of kilter.

"You did ask the question," said John by way of explanation.

James lifted his pint glass, noted that it was already empty. He put it down and checked his watch.

"Shit! Is that the time?! Oh bloody hell! I better get back!"

James slipped from his chair and grabbed his bag. By some feat of professional bar keeping, John was at the door of the pub to see him out. James strode to the door and before leaving he turned to say goodbye to Sean. Of the man, there was no sign.

6

James turned to John.

"Goodbye James," said the bar man, his expression implacable, it contained a strange finality.

James wanted to enquire after Sean. He felt. Odd. Instead he walked out into the blinding daylight, feeling like a prisoner being unexpectedly released out into the big wide world, bewildered, cautious and dizzy. He turned back. The door was firmly shut and the pub contained no signs of life as though the whole episode within the Red Lion with Sean and John had never taken place.

59

# 7

"**I**s it like being drunk?" James asked Melissa this question completely out of the blue.

Later, he would understand just how tactless and bad he was being and later still, as he nursed a hangover he would get the punchline. He would understand where Sean had been coming from, although he would still harbour feelings of some strange mysticism around that entire counter. It wasn't just the alcohol, something was going on in that pub and something was going on with Sean.

Curiously, James didn't go back to the Red Lion and over time he doubted he would ever find it, so he consigned it to legend.

Melissa eyed her husband, "I take it it didn't go well with Simon then?"

She'd never been a fan of Simon. What Melissa saw in Simon was a bully. Simon was a rubbish caricature of a spoilt brat. He didn't share his toys and he had no qualms about burning people. He took what he wanted and had a callous and brutish nature. And that was on his good days, as far as she was concerned. She'd never wanted James to get into bed with the man, and she could see the conclusion of their so-called friendship from a mile off. One day, Simon would abuse and use James and James would limp away, damaged and very much down on the deal. Simon needed James, James had never needed Simon, but he couldn't see that.

"Why do you say that?" asked James defensively.

"You seem a little worse for wear, which isn't at all like you," said Melissa gently.

James shrugged, "It'll be fine."

"In answer to your question," Melissa sighed, "Probably. A bit. I dunno."

James grabbed her hand clumsily and squeezed, "I love you."

He managed to slur the three little worlds comically and it was all Melissa could do not to laugh.

"The memory loss you might have as a result of your post-Simon beers," Melissa nodded, "that is kind of similar."

She slumped a little as she thought about it a little more, "the hangover too. The horrible feeling of something happening that shouldn't have, that you've done something bad, but can't even remember it. Then it..."

Her chin creased as she fought tears. James got up and raced around the dining room table, catching his hip on the corner of the table, "Shit! Ow!" He grabbed her and held her.

"I'm OK," Melissa eventually said having collapsed into James' arms and cried, "it's knowing that there's more to come and I'm a passenger. The frustration and the… all of it I suppose."

James gave her a squeeze, "Cuppa?"

She smiled through her tears and nodded.

James boiled the kettle and milled around the kitchen sorting the mugs, tea bags and milk. Melissa watched her husband's deliberate movements. He didn't get drunk often and it was funny watching him make a concerted effort not to appear drunk, only to make it very clear with his exaggerated and theatrical movements that he was quite, quite drunk.

Teas made, he returned to the table and they sat alongside each other. Melissa wrapped her hands around the warm mug, "I'll tell you what it's like, you drunk fool." She was grinning now, "You know when you read down a page in a book and yet when you get to the end you realise nothing is in your head?"

James nodded. He'd done that all too often and the sensation of having lost something, of something so simple just not working was daunting.

"Well, when that happened to me…"

James noticed the use of past tense and it caused him pain.

There was a resignation in that. This was talk of a time past and there was no going back.

"...I would have another set of thoughts in my head that had displaced the words from the page. I'd be thinking about work, or what I was going to make for dinner. My mind would be elsewhere. Do you get that?"

James nodded again, "Yeah, that same thing happens to me, the words on the page... I've read them and I'm not listening to them because I'm too focused on something else."

Melissa smiled, "so although it's a bit crap and disconcerting, you find an explanation for what went wrong and then you head back up the page. You can find where it was that you left off when you started thinking about something else. You find your thread, don't you?"

James chuckled despite the gravity of the conversation, "You're right. I've never properly thought about it, but now that I do, that's how it works!"

Melissa's expression changed, it was like a dark cloud passing over her face, "In my case, there is no other focus. There are no thoughts of work or dinner ingredients. There's nothing there."

"Oh," said James, he put his mug down. He felt sick as he thought about how that must feel.

Melissa took a deep, ragged breath and went on, "So, I've gone to the end of the page and words haven't gone in. Or they've gone in, but I realise that they aren't there. We're creatures of habit, so we'll head back up the page to find..." she paused, took another of those deep, ragged breaths, "there is no page, James. There's no book. All of it is gone. The book isn't there anymore and you don't know what you're doing, you don't know what's happening with you anymore. There's nothing. And there's the frustration of knowing there shouldn't be nothing. It's wrong and its horrible and life as you once knew it isn't there anymore."

James reached out for Melissa, but she raised her hand.

"I know you shouldn't ask me questions like this and I can see why. But I'm glad you did and I'm glad I can at least answer you right now. What's frightening is that I have these two separate lives. There's my former life that I'm trying desperately to hold onto and then there's this invading nothingness that I know will eventually take over until there's nothing left of me."

Melissa's body shook as she fought the tears.

"Melissa?" James said it quietly and with the seriousness usually reserved for a child.

Melissa turned towards him and tried to read his face.

"I love you more in this moment than I ever thought possible," there were tears brimming in his eyes.

She punched him playfully on the arm, fought the urge to tell him it was the drink talking. She knew it wasn't, instead, "why? Why would you want this and what's ahead?!"

He answered simply, "because it's you."

"It's not though is it!?"

"Yes it is! If either of us had any doubts about that? Well. You. Here and now. That's you more than at any other time I've known you."

Melissa took his hand, "are you sure you want to do this?"

"Positive," he smiled.

"Why James? Why?"

"Because we have time. Because I will get to know you in a way few husbands get to know their wives. We will spend this time together and we'll talk and get to know each other. This is a wake-up call. This is our time."

"But..."

"No! No, buts. There's loads that I don't know about you."

James got up, suddenly animated. "That's it!" he exclaimed, scurrying from the kitchen.

Melissa watched him go, wondering what he was up to. She

heard drawers opening and closing and her husband muttering to himself. Then she heard the sounds of his approach.

"There!"

He sat at the table and before him he had placed an A4 notepad and a biro.

Melissa's brow creased, "what?" she asked him, because whatever he was up to was not at all clear to her.

"You're going to tell me all about you and I'm going to take notes!" beamed James.

"You're what?"

James turned to her, "your long term memory is fine. It will be fine. It's where the both of us can spend time and I *want* to. I want to know you inside out. I want to be with you every step of the way, so bear with me, OK? If I have a pen and paper and I jot stuff down... it's how I work I suppose."

Melissa smiled curiously, "so you're not going to write my autobiography though?"

James winked a clumsy drunk wink, "well I might!"

He earned another punch to his arm for that.

# 8

There were many good days.

Mostly the good days were punctuated with what they liked to refer to as hiccups. The hiccups were mostly innocuous. The problem was that hiccups can appear at any point in time and they come unannounced and sometimes they really pick their moments.

One time, they were in the local supermarket. James and Melissa had a habit of drifting away from each other as they shopped. One of them would spot something they wanted to take a closer look at and the other would continue, grabbing provisions along the way. Their main objective, as well as getting everything they needed (so they wouldn't have to make a second trip), was to get the hell out of the supermarket as quickly as possible. Supermarket shopping experiences were not the best and there were a thousand things they would both rather be doing, like degreasing the oven or tackling the weeds behind the shed at the bottom of the garden.

James had done what he had done hundreds of times before, he'd gone down the aisle picking up tins of baked beans, foregoing his favourite brand and choosing Melissa's and then on to the tinned tomatoes. Along he went to the packs of rice and lentils and then he was off round the corner and heading up the next aisle, grabbing eggs as he went. Melissa had taken an interest in the herbs and spices. She knew they were short on a few and she also wanted to add to their collection so they had more options when they both cooked. Both of them liked to cook and there was something infuriating about opening a cupboard and not finding all of the ingredients, worse still, directly after a *big shop.* When you'd gone through the pain of a *big shop* you were supposed to be stocked up on everything. Only after the best part of a week were you to find yourself scrabbling around in the fridge and the cupboards and innovating to ensure the food nearing its use-by date was eaten.

Melissa turned away from the shelves of herbs and spices to say something to James about the coriander. She couldn't remember whether they had a whole jar of the herb and besides, there was nothing better than the fresh stuff, but would they actually use much of it? They would have to plan a meal or three to incorporate it. She was sure they did pots of the live stuff. It was a shame that between them, they would fail to water the pot and the remaining coriander would wilt and die on the window sill. The sad demise of the plant pot would be rendered tragic as it sat in the shadow of the dripping kitchen tap. So near and yet so far.

Melissa turned towards where she thought James was. Where, in her world, James *was.* She could feel his presence just to her right and slightly behind her.

68

8

"Have we got coriander?" she smiled.

She felt a jolt run through her as she realised that the person she was talking to was not James.

This was not James.

"Oh! I'm sorry, I thought you were my husband!" she apologised to the stranger.

In reply, the stranger smiled at her uncertainly and quickly moved away.

"Only you can't be, because..." Melissa said to the retreating figure, she added the final words more quietly, "...you're a woman."

Melissa looked down the aisle beyond the woman. No sign of James. Then she looked behind her. Then she turned back to the herbs and spices and she froze.

Where was she?

Why was she here?

The world around her blurred and she felt this inexplicable feeling of abandonment and detachment. In this moment, she had no words for the things around her or the way she felt. A detachment from the world around her. An absence. Only, the absence was being filled with waves of emotion and in the midst of the overwhelming emotion she stood, isolated,

69

confused and upset.

This was the way James found her.

The change in his wife was shattering and it was as much as he could do not to join her in paralysis. As it was, he stood for a moment, unable to act or speak. This was probably just as well as had he rushed in, it could have gone all the worse for both of them.

He wasn't quite sure how he unlocked the situation, he just did.

James left the trolley where it was, that was no longer important. All that mattered was getting Melissa out of here and home. Somehow, he had touched her then guided her all the while talking softly and reassuringly to her. She hadn't said a word. She'd just come with him. Climbed into the car and come home with him.

At some point his wife had returned and the hiccup was over.

Later, James had almost laughed to himself as he thought Melissa had now gotten out of the supermarket run, the joy of shopping was now his and his alone. Thankfully, there was another way and the following day he'd sat with Melissa and shared the easier task of compiling their first online shop. They'd get the bulk of their provisions delivered from now on. A simple adjustment to make things work in their new life.

It was all about finding adjustments and solutions.

James could do that and he would willingly do so.

Nonetheless, a spectre hung over the both of them, it was the constant reminder that the good days would dwindle and life would get more difficult. That they were largely passengers on this journey and the concept of free will was a bit of a joke right now.

Only...

*Baby, life's what you make it*

James had taken to playing music from past decades, random selections of tunes they had grown up with. Sometimes the music seemed to do its thing in the background and left them to it. James knew this wasn't quite true and the music was stirring them gently. Other times, the music would grab one of them and take them to another time and another place.

Often, tears would come unbidden. Seldom were the tears weighted with sadness, quite the opposite. The tears were a celebration of their life. A celebration of times past and golden memories that in turn highlighted their lives right now.

At first, they would ask each other awkward questions.

"Are you OK?"

"What's up?"

"What are you thinking about?"

The sorts of questions that teenagers ask each other in the early throws of the dating game. In a way, they were back in the early stages of a new relationship because the rules had changed from underneath them. They were spending time with each other and learning how to share that time. Lapsing more and more into companionable silences that were a product of true sharing.

James realised that he had lapsed into a state of *being busy* prior to this concerted effort to spend time with his wife and share it fully. That he had shared space with her, but not time. They had had a carefully choreographed life that revolved around work and their own needs. They hadn't spent all that much time truly together. Oh, they had been there in the same space, but they had been separate somehow. They hadn't given of themselves and this had been evident in that first stage of awkwardness.

They were learning how to relax in each other's company.

As well as the tears flowing freely when the mood took them, they also sang. The first time had been terrible, they were so out of practice. But they had laughed and they had kept laughing in that way that people insist on referring to as school kid laughter. The uncontrollable laughter that cannot be stopped. A laughter with a mind of its own that will go on and on until you learn to accept it and then embrace it. Maybe it's referred to as school kid laughter because adults work so hard to avoid these bursts of self-expression, they are so careful to control themselves and manage what everyone sees, that they lose something of themselves along the way. One thing was

72

for certain, James was finding himself and getting to know his wife all over again.

The music was playing throughout the downstairs of their home, but of James there was no sign. He was squirrelled away in the smallest downstairs room with the door shut. Melissa was under strict orders to stay out until he was finished and then and only then, would he invite her in. She had no idea what he was up to. She didn't think that he was reorganising the furniture in the room and there had been no deliveries that she was aware of. She was intrigued, all the more so because James had smiled an enigmatic smile and there had been a mischievous twinkle in his eye as he had closed the door on her and told her to keep out, like a naughty schoolboy retreating into his den.

The anticipation of what James was up to had gotten too much and Melissa resorted to sneaking up to the door and pressing an ear to it. She was sorely tempted to fetch a tumbler, all the better to hear what was going on behind that door. There were no dramatic sounds. Nothing to give away the activity within. Muted sounds of movement and the occasional... what was that? A rustle of paper? James cleared his throat on the other side of the door and Melissa darted away from it quickly for fear of being caught snooping.

The door opened and Melissa froze. Caught in the act and guilty as hell.

"Oh aye!?" said James in mock admonishment.

"I was just... erm... passing," said Melissa weakly.

"And your ear just happened to brush the door, eh?" winked James.

Melissa shifted her weight from one foot to the other. She'd been caught bang to rights. James smiled, she looked like a little girl lost. Seeing his smile, she attempted a peek over his shoulder.

"Oh no you don't!" he laughed, "close your eyes, or you'll ruin the surprise!"

She scowled, but did as she was told. He moved around her and slipped his hands over her eyes. He was close and moved in closer still.

"You know I love you, right?" he whispered in her ear.

Melissa smiled, from where he was, he couldn't see it, but he felt it and he heard it in her voice, "yes. And I love you too."

"Good," said James all business-like again, "so no peeking."

He gently walked her into the room.

"Ready?" he whispered.

"Yes," she replied.

He removed his hands, but she kept her eyes closed. She

8

instinctively knew that that was what was required. She felt him move away from her and briefly missed that closeness, knew he was now in front of her. Watching her. She liked that. She could feel his smile and his warmth towards her.

"OK, you can open your eyes now."

James watched as his wife opened her eyes. He had a fleeting moment of panic which he hated for taking something of the joy from him. Just for a second, he thought he spied an absence and he thought he'd always be watching Melissa for signs that all was not right in her world, but then she lit up and all was more than right in her world and in his. She clapped her hands gleefully as she looked around the room.

"But how...!?"

The walls were covered in photos.

Melissa couldn't remember the last time she had had a photo developed. That had been a ritual when she was young. Photos were taken on a reel of twenty four or thirty six and you felt blessed if you got another couple of photos out of that reel. Mostly photos were taken on special occasions or on holiday and then it was a case of a special trip to the chemists to have the photos developed. Only then would you see whether the photo had come out OK. There was something precious and special about those images. There was a care and almost a ceremony to them.

How quickly had they all moved on to a state where the facility

75

to capture images was ever present? No longer were people restricted to twenty four images, they could take hundreds and thousands of photos, but as a result the capturing of images was throw away and anything special was drowned in the thousands of images that were so readily dismissible.

James had had photos made of images throughout Melissa's past. Not just their shared past, but from when she was a little girl. Some of the photos were originals, he'd not had to print those, but how had he got them?

"You did all this?" she asked him.

"Well, I contacted a few people so there were photos from throughout your life and you can always add more. I'm sure there's more if we do some digging and ask around?"

She threw her arms around him and hugged him hard, "thank you!"

He hugged her back, his voice quivering with emotion, "I wanted a place for you. That... you know. You can go and you have your memories right there in front of you."

"You've made me a memory room! I love it!" she said these words against his ear and punctuated them with kisses.

She kept on kissing and he turned his face and kissed her right back.

# 9

L ater, as they lay sprawled on the sofa together enjoying a glow that couples sometimes take the time to enjoy after they've spent time enjoying each other, James extricated himself from Melissa and from the sofa and stood and stretched.

"Cup of tea?" he suggested.

"That would be nice," Melissa agreed.

He returned with two mugs of tea. He may have asked if she wanted a cup, but they'd always used mugs. He handed her her mug. They both had their own mugs, several of them for the rounds of tea they may have in any particular day.

"How very British," she grinned at James, having taken a sip of her tea.

"Yes, rather," James put on a stiff-upper-lipped matinee idol voice.

They sat in silence drinking their tea and then Melissa broke the silence.

"You know, I thought you'd got me a puppy..." she ventured.

"A puppy?"

James was taken aback. He'd not been expecting that. He'd not even considered it. His face went from surprise to sadness.

Melissa saw the change, "I don't suppose we can have a puppy now, can we?"

James sighed, he couldn't lie. He couldn't sugar coat it. Life could be an utter git and right now, in the aftermath of such a lovely time, it was doing it's git thing. Introducing an idea and an idea that was beautiful and wonderful at that, and then shooting it down in flames, right in front of them.

What was more beautiful and wonderful than a puppy?

The thing was with puppies and many of the big things in life, people never really thought about the hard work and the less beautiful and wonderful aspects of those big things. It was just as well, or people just wouldn't do most of the big things in life and they would miss out as a result. The point was to celebrate the best in something and then launch yourself into it so that the work and the less pleasant aspects *just were.* No one minded those things because... PUPPY! That mad exuberance took a person, and a puppy, a long, long way.

James and Melissa didn't have that luxury anymore, and that

made James feel like a complete and utter shit. He felt like the worst kind of party pooper and buzz killer ever. It hurt all the more because he could see Melissa with a puppy and he knew it would be good for her. How could it not be? Right now, his mind's eye was providing him with a visual of Melissa with a small, golden Labrador puppy on her lap. The little blighter was mouthy and was chewing her finger with its tiny, pin like teeth and Melissa was laughing. The sound of her laughter was joyous.

There was a shadow cast right across this though.

A big *what if.*

Terrible, grey and dread words filed through James' mind. Words like *it's irresponsible.*

And Melissa was looking at James and seeing their reality writ large across his face.

He shrugged, "there's more than one way to skin a cat."

As soon as he said the words he regretted them. He felt like he was digging a hole. Making matters worse.

"A cat?"

"No, sorry, we can't..."

Melissa looked even more glum. Well done, James, he thought to himself.

"I suppose we can't have a cat either," she said sadly.

"No, I'm allergic to them remember?"

This was actually a slight step up and away from the doom and gloom.

She smiled, she actually smiled, "Oh yes! The nose bleeds and pustules!"

"Alright!" protested James, "it's not funny!"

His cat allergy was a corker though.

"Anyway," said Melissa, rationalising the cat angle, "cats are evil bastards. Not sure I want to introduce even more evil into our lives right now."

It was said with levity, but a weight fell upon the room as the words settled.

They drank the rest of their tea in companionable silence, lost in their thoughts and not wanting to give voice to those thoughts. There were dark and choppy seas ahead and beyond that who knew what.

# 10

He didn't know how he got there.

He seemed to be making a habit of drifting into places and then wondering how he'd managed it.

Even when he thought about it later, he would not come to understand how it came to be, but he was glad that it happened. He liked to think there were forces beyond his comprehension and on this particular day, someone or something was looking out for him and gave him a gentle shove in the right direction.

He was strung out with stress. A stress beyond anything he had ever known. He was exhausted. Dead on his feet. Caught in a cycle of stress and sleep deprivation that was making him sick. Sick with worry. He knew he needed to break out of it, but didn't know how. Knowing he should and not seeing any way he could, only added to his burden.

He thought he was close to breaking point and the prospect of that eventuality frightened him. He was all there was and without him... well, he didn't know how that one would pan out, only that it would not make for a happy ending.

He'd thought that he'd understood his granddad and the way his life had ended. He hadn't known the half of it, not until now. Not until he was walking in his shoes and struggling to put one foot in front of the other.

Maybe it was his granddad, or at least thoughts of his granddad that brought him to this place...

"Hello?"

James didn't respond. That single word had broken his dark reverie but brought him all the way back into the present. He remained dazed.

"Can I help you?"

The voice was warm and comforting. Those words not often said in a way that conveyed that the person uttering them actually meant them.

James looked at the woman who was enquiring as to whether she could help him for the first time. She was wearing blue and the shade of blue and the cut of the trousers and the top marked her out as a nurse of some sort. The voice indicated a bedside manner that was genuine and caring.

Despite himself, James looked at his surroundings for the very first time and took them in. He knew this wasn't going to do him any favours and could potentially give rise to some concern. The woman before him would see that James wasn't with it and could potentially present a danger to her and this place.

There wasn't anything else for it. James was running on empty and all he had was honesty.

"My wife..." he began, but he didn't know what to say. Even now.

The woman in front of him smiled kindly, "do you fancy a cuppa?"

He laughed. Couldn't help it and as he laughed he realised he was crying and had been crying for a while now. All he could do was smile by way of a reply.

* * *

"There, that's better isn't it?"

And it was.

There was something comforting about a mug of tea and the casual ritual surrounding it. If someone offered you a brew, it conferred some of the simple and easy elements of friendship combined with quiet and calm. You could talk over a brew, or you could have a spot of quiet.

It started with the spot of quiet. James needed that and it was obvious he needed that to the other occupant of the room. They were in a small office, but both sat this side of the desk that filled half of the space. Although the room was small, there was enough space between them for it not to be too cosy.

James looked up from the warm mug he was cupping protectively in both hands and he saw the woman for the first time. Saw her properly with his mind as well as his eyes. Even then, it was debatable whether he saw her. Really saw her. For what he saw was the nurse's uniform and in seeing that he knew where he was. The why of it was not so straightforward, but he thought he knew. Somehow, deep down, he knew this was where he needed to be and his beleaguered body had brought him here for... what? Respite, he supposed. Time out in a place where things might make a sort of sense to him.

It was a care home. It wasn't the care home that his grandparents had spent the last days of their lives in, that was up the other end of the country. Neither was it the care home Melissa's grandma had stayed in. That building was long gone, demolished to make way for a haulage yard.

James had gravitated to a nearby care home when it had all gotten a bit much. What now though? He was here, but he didn't have a clue as to what to do. As this occurred to him, he thought of himself as an intruder. If a bewildered bloke had stumbled into his office building, would James have made him a cuppa and sat him down so he could compose himself?

No, was the resounding answer to that one.

How many places would welcome a confused James, he wondered. Not many was the obvious answer. He had fluked the right place, at the right time and with the right person. He doubted many care home nurses would have treated him with such understanding, let alone had the time to give him.

"Thanks," he said simply.

"It's fine," the woman smiled kindly, "I was going on my break anyway, it's nice to share a brew with someone."

She raised her mug and smiled again.

James thought back to his arrival, an arrival that had taken place only a matter of minutes ago, but seemed so far away now.

"I mentioned my wife, didn't I?" he heard his own words and inwardly cringed. He was not doing brand *James* any favours at all. He was a young, strong bloke and yet here he was sounding weak and all at sea. He supposed that was exactly what he was and he didn't have the energy or wherewithal to do anything about that right now.

"You did," confirmed the woman.

The woman.

"Sorry!" James said this a little too enthusiastically and the step change in his energy and demeanour startled the woman, "Sorry..." he said a little more calmly, "I don't even know your name." He extended his hand, "mine's James."

She looked at his hand for a moment and then reached out and shook it. Her hand shake was firm and surprisingly strong, "I'm Helen."

"Helen, I like that name," he cocked his head back slightly, thinking, "you know what, I don't think I know a Helen. Knew a few when I was a kid, but never encountered one since. Isn't that strange?"

"Not at all," Helen chuckled, "Helen seems like a bit of a common name doesn't it? But it went out of fashion after my parents named me. You don't hear a bunch of names these days, the Sharons and the Tracys, all replaced by Kylies and Chardonnays I suppose."

James smiled despite himself, "yeah, my name has been customised, mostly it's Jamies these days."

"Some of the old names have come back though, so it isn't all bad. Alfies, Bettys, Reginalds and Connies."

"Makes up for the terrible spellings of names to make them unique I suppose."

"I'm not sure that some parents even get that they've come up with an alternative spelling. I blame text speak and all that nonsense, I bet there's kids called Yolo out there somewhere. Can't imagine an eighty year old here and calling them Yolo!"

"Yolo?" asked James.

Helen rolled her eyes, "you only live once."

"Ah," said James as the penny dropped.

They both lapsed into silence. James was thinking about that fine sentiment and how it applied to Melissa and him right now. Then he thought about what Helen may be thinking. You only live once. In an old people's care home.

They, the fabled *they* who may or may not be the *silent majority*, called them care homes or old people's homes. These were places where families took their old people to be taken care of because those old people could no longer take care of themselves.

Suddenly, a part of James didn't want to be here. Wasn't this where Melissa would end up, or a place like it? A weird form of child prodigy thrust forth into a world made for older people. Out of place, and somewhere she didn't really belong, but there was nowhere else for her to go. This was it.

Hobson's choice.

"My wife," started James, not knowing where he would go after those two opening words, but knowing that he should talk and that maybe this was a place that he *could* talk, "she's like the inmates here."

"Inmates?!" Helen looked indignant, but strangely, she was also smiling.

James gave her a puzzled look. Had he referred to the people in the care home as inmates? Well, now the cat was out of the bag, he supposed that they were. They were stuck here until the grim reaper came and collected them. There was no escaping this place, and even if they had the wherewithal to escape, where would they go and what would they do? There wasn't a nearby pool filled with alien eggs that would magically rejuvenate them. Besides, that film had skipped over the biggest part of growing old, it had focused on the actors ageing bodies, but James didn't remember the mental aspect of growing old in that film...

...actually, when he came to think of it, he did.

The old people in that film. The ones who's minds had aged. They were write offs. Oh, they covered this off neatly. There were those who were old at heart. They had gone too far and they were no longer youthful. In the background though, there were the *others.* The ones who didn't even have a choice and didn't count. They didn't have any lines, they weren't even extras, they were background scenery. There was no cure for them. Not even alien eggs that had almost magical, restorative properties were a cure for dementia. That was a message in the film that James only now got. The aliens could only offer a second crack at life to those who were young at heart and who hadn't been ravaged by an irreversible brain disease. It had been there in plain sight and yet James had chosen to skip right past it and focus on the feel good aspects of the film. It was no consolation that her was not alone and that pretty much everyone else did this.

Helen seemed to take pity on James, "I've heard them called a variety of things over the years, but inmates is a new one. You'll get me in trouble you know!"

"How so?" asked James.

"Well, now you've introduced me to this exciting new word for our *residents* I'll end up using it. I just hope I don't say it in earshot of the wrong ears…"

"Oops," James cringed, "I'm not sure why I said that," he offered by way of explanation.

"Well, in a way, it's not far off the mark is it?"

"It's not nice though is it?" said James.

"No. No it isn't," agreed Helen, "but then what is nice about this?"

James hadn't expected that and his expression said it all.

Helen frowned at him, "you didn't think I'd work here all these years and not see what it is that we do as a society and what this last stage of life is really like do you?"

James shrugged, he didn't know what he thought because he'd never taken the time to think about it. That was a shaming revelation.

"You have to understand something to deal with it properly.

Or you at least have to try. My... *job,*" she said this in a way that conveyed that what she did here certainly wasn't a job, "like any job, has aspects I'd really rather not do, but then if I don't do them, then who will... no. No, that's not right. When I first walked into the business end of a care home I didn't know what I'd let myself in for. I was young and I didn't know what I was letting myself in for. We all do that don't we?"

James smiled and nodded. He'd certainly done it.

"When people ask me what I do, I know they only ever think about the mopping up that I do. The mechanics of the job. They miss the bit that makes all the difference. To them and to me. These are *people,* James. They have lived longer than you and I, and they have seen things and done things that we can only ever dream about. After only a very short while, I discovered the rewards of being here. The mystery of another human being. None of us see that special person across a crowded room and instantly think about them doing a poo, do we?"

"I..." James was taken aback.

Helen laughed, "sorry, that's my humour right there, and the way I make sense of what I do. I have to make sense of it, because few other people do. Care homes are a solution to a problem and the problem is old people. That's really sad, because so many people miss out on what these people still have left to give," she shrugged, the shrug said that this was life. Go figure.

Helen fixed James with a stare, it was intense, but also held a warmth to it, "when you say your wife is like the... residents... here, I'm guessing there isn't a significant age gap between you both and that you're not much older than you look?"

James shook his head, his voice broke in the midst of the words he spoke, "she's younger than me!"

He cleared his throat, "sorry, frog in my throat."

Helen nodded, "you'll get a few of those, I expect."

Busted.

"Early onset dementia?" she asked, her voice quiet and suddenly very serious.

James nodded.

"Bastard isn't it?"

James wasn't sure how to respond.

"Life," said Helen by way of explanation, "it's a complete and utter bastard. I think the sooner we get that, the sooner we can just get on and make the most of the moments when it's being a bit less of a bastard."

"It's the simple things..." began James.

"Yes, enjoy those," agreed Helen.

"No, she... the other day she thought I'd got her a puppy..."

"Oh..." said Helen.

"And that would be reckless and unfair of me to do that, wouldn't it?" his eyes were pleading, as though he wanted Helen to disagree with him and tell him no, it was OK to get a puppy, because everyone else just went ahead and did it. Mostly at Christmas and by New Year's Day, what with hangovers and the start of another depressing year, the novelty was already wearing off and down to the dog's trust they went in their droves.

Instead Helen nodded agreement, it would be reckless to get a puppy, but then she said something that made a lot of sense and gave James some hope.

# 11

**M**elissa looked confused.

This time James was not worried about her confusion because he was the cause of the confusion, or rather the architect of it. The focus of her confusion was the big, saggy bag of big bones and silky, furry hide sitting next to James.

Melissa had just encountered Milo for the very first time and Milo was sitting on her usual seat on the sofa, next to James. Milo returned Melissa's look of confusion with a trademark hangdog expression. As well as big bones, he had huge, expressive eyes. Eyes that grabbed Melissa's attention and then held onto it like a tractor beam.

There was a chicken and egg thing going on with Milo. Was he a needy, seeker of attention first and foremost, his eyes and their enthralling ways aiding and abetting his needs, or was it always about the eyes and the rest of it an inevitable state of affairs if you possessed eyes such as his?

Milo spoke to Melissa, as much as a dog can speak, he did. As well as possessing wonderful eyes, Milo was vocal. He wasn't going to rely upon his eyes alone, not with these fickle human creatures. It paid to capture their attention in as many different ways as was possible.

"Is he speaking to me?" asked Melissa, her eyebrows still broadcasting her confusion.

"Yes, apparently he does that," said James, the hint of a smile on his face.

Melissa took a couple of steps closer to Milo, still unsure as to what was happening here, "James, what have you done?" she said, attempting stern words, but there was too much merriment peeking through those words and lighting up her face.

"Arooo! Aroooowoo!" said Milo.

He cocked his head to one side and continued to urge Melissa closer. He was going all out for a fuss now, his tail was wagging and his front feet were padding up and down on the spot in anticipation of a fuss.

"Is he...?" she began.

"Doing the Princess of Hearts eye thing? Yeah..." said James, he was grinning now.

Then Melissa closed the gap between them and gave Milo a good head rub, focusing around his ears and eliciting an appreciative, low rumble from the dog.

"He won't let you stop now you've started, you know. He only let me stop when you walked in," explained James.

Melissa looked over at James, "what's his name?"

"Milo," said James.

"Hello, Milo!" said Melissa, redoubling her efforts to give him a fuss.

Milo returned the greeting with a short howl.

"He's a character!" exclaimed Melissa.

"He certainly is," agreed James.

"But we can't keep him... can we?" now Melissa was attempting Milo's eye trick.

"No," said James firmly, "no we can't."

The expression on Melissa's face was almost too much for James. He felt a wave of unexpected emotion and also felt awful about potentially upsetting her.

He winked at her, hoping this would head anything bad off at the pass.

"James, why are you doing that weird wink thing?" she asked, now very suspicious as to what was going on.

"Well," said James, puffing out a dramatic breath as a prelude to his explanation of the arrangement he agreed with Milo, "we're not going to keep him. We do have to give him back to his owners. Only... then we get to collect him again for more Milo time."

"We have a time share dog?" said Melissa, trying to make sense of it.

"I hadn't thought about it like that, but yes. Yes we do. There's a website and an app and you can spend time with dogs whose owners need a bit of help when they are out of the house, so everyone, as they say, is a winner."

"And you chose Milo?"

Melissa said this in an inscrutable way. This left James wondering whether, in Melissa's final analysis, he had done good or instead missed the mark with his choice of dog.

"Yes, well, I..." he began. He'd so wanted Melissa to like Milo. Didn't she see how bloody good the dog was?

"James," Melissa said in a matter-of-fact way, "Milo smells funky."

"Yes, well, Bassets do have a certain distinctive bouquet, it's a part of what makes the breed. You get used to it apparently..."

11

"He probably drools," she added.

"Lots of dogs drool... it's what they do when they're hungry, Melissa!" James was feeling a tad defensive now.

"I bet he moults loads too."

"No... well, he'll moult, but not drifts and drifts of the stuff. Most dogs moult."

"Labradoodles don't."

"Ah! That's where you're wrong! That depends on their coat!" said James triumphantly, he'd won a point.

"Of course it depends on their coats!" laughed Melissa.

"No, labradoodles can have one of three coats. Some labradoodles moult and others don't... Did you want a labradoodle?"

Melissa laughed again, then she hugged Milo and gave him an even bigger fuss. James watched her stroking and hugging the soppy Basset and him lapping it up, rumbling with contended noises and his back leg twitching up and down involuntarily as Melissa found that sweet spot that all dogs have. She was talking and chuckling and didn't seem to have a care in the world.

It seemed that Milo was a hit and just as importantly, that Melissa was a hit with Milo. James hadn't thought that would be an issue, but you never could tell. He'd learnt not to expect interactions to be foregone successes, that chemistry had to be there for it to work and you could never second guess chemistry.

Melissa sat back from her fuss making.

"So, you're OK with our visitor then?" asked James.

"What do you think?" she grinned.

"And all that stuff about drool and moulting?"

"I was winding you up, you fool!" she laughed and looked set to hug him, except a big paw tapped her forearm and the tap was followed up with a plaintive rumble.

"Aroooo!" said Milo, not liking Melissa's switch of attention.

"Milo you silly dog!" Melissa ruffled the folds of skin under his chin and he dropped his head in an attempt to keep her hand exactly where it was.

"I think he has the measure of you already," James smiled.

"And you too," laughed Melissa.

Milo had placed a possessive paw on James' thigh. James was going nowhere. He reached out and scratched behind Milo's ear.

"Shall we take him for a walk around the block?" asked James.

Melissa looked up at him, "yes, let's..."

He got up and padded over to the kitchen. Melissa heard the tell-tale rustling of a shopping bag and got up to investigate, Milo leaving the sofa with a grace and agility that was surprising for such a chunky dog, he padded alongside her, not wanting to be left alone. They would discover that, once he'd settled, he could sleep for England and that he could occupy the entirety of the sofa as he stretched out. He developed a habit of kicking James while he slept. Even if Melissa and James swapped seats, it was always James that he kicked as he dreamt about chasing rabbits. Milo continued to be vocal even when aslumber, but none of it was obtrusive, there was something endearing and comforting about the background noises he provided. James and Melissa quickly noticed Milo's absences from the house, their home felt a little empty without him lounging, or padding around and demanding their attention in the best of ways, and that was his skill, he made people want to be the subject of his demands for his demands were always easily met and enjoyably so.

As Melissa entered the kitchen, James looked up from two shopping bags, one worn and well used, the other new. He reached into the older bag and waved a chewed toy bone.

"There you go, mate!"

James dropped the chew toy in front of Milo. Milo ignored it completely and kept his eyes trained on James. Where there were shopping bags there was the promise of food and treats and interesting smells and tastes. There were no flies on Milo, he watched the bags intently.

James straightened, "this bag is a few things from Milo's owners so he has some semblance of familiarity," he pointed to the corner of the kitchen, "apparently he sometimes likes to take himself away from everyone and chill on a bed..."

"So you bought him a bed?" asked Melissa.

"Well, yeah," James shrugged, "and it's got a blanket on it from his other home."

Melissa smiled warmly and kissed James, "you're a softy after all!"

James shrugged again, "well I thought I'd best make him comfortable..."

Melissa paused, straightened up and put her hands on her hips, "hang on buster! What if I'd not gone along with this plan of yours!?"

"My plan!? The cheek of her! Can you hear her, Milo?! She was the one with the pouty lip and big eyes at the thought of a puppy! I do all this hard work, find the biggest puppy imaginable and surprise her with this fine figure of a dog, for you are a fine, fine figure of a dog, Milo..." he crouched down and rubbed Milo's head, sending folds of skin all over his face, "...and she has a go! Well, I don't know about you, but I'm going for a walk. Are you coming Milo?"

James reached into the new bag and searched around before retrieving a lead. He brandished it enthusiastically.

"Walkies!"

Milo looked from the lead to James and barked once. A deep and loud bark that came up from the ground and rattled the ribs as it travelled upwards. James swore he heard the windows rattle in their frames too. The dog had a powerful bark. But nowhere as powerful as his will. He sat down heavily and whined.

"Not so sure he's up for a walk," observed Melissa.

"OK, OK," James was struggling with the tag on the lead, it was attached with a piece of belligerent plastic that was currently cutting into his skin and turning his index finger a worrying hue of purple.

"Good job he's not going mad for a walk while you faff with the packaging on the new lead!" chortled Melissa.

"You're not helping," said James, a slightly dry edge to his words.

He stopped his hurried attempts at sorting Milo's lead. Instead he looked at the dog seated before him. Milo looked meaningfully at the object in James' hand and whined again for maximum effect. The whine wasn't a whine of positive anticipation. The whine, together with Milo's body language said to James, *what are you doing!? Whatever it is, it needs to stop!*

James sighed, then he walked over to the draw in the kitchen that contained three pairs of scissors. He retrieved the one pair that could actually cut through industrial grade plastic tags and packaging. James supposed that those scissors cut through bone, if he ever needed to use a pair of scissors to cut bone that was. He hoped that that eventuality would never come to pass.

James walked to the bin and dropped the plastic into the recycling, then he came full circle to return to the unmoved and seemingly immovable Milo.

Raising the lead for all to see he said quietly, "you don't want a walk, do you?"

Milo tilted his head to one side and gave James a look. The looks said *what do you think?*

"How did you get him here?" Melissa asked.

"Car," answered James.

"Ah," Melissa said.

James turned to look at her.

She shrugged, "seems that Milo isn't a fan of walking."

"But *all* dogs love walking! That's one of the few things they love! Food. Chewing things. Being stroked. Sleeping. Walking! People get dogs so they can go on walks! Have we just got the only dog in Dog World who doesn't like walks?!"

"Didn't the owners say anything?"

James stroked his chin, "they said he didn't need much exercise."

"There you go then."

Melissa saw that James was crestfallen, "why don't you take him into the garden."

"Good idea. Come on Milo!"

The dog just looked at the strange human as he walked towards the back door.

"James?"

"Yes?"

"I'd put the lead away so Milo can't see it?"

James looked at the lead in his hand. He walked back to the bag of goodies he'd bought for Milo and placed it inside, out of sight. Immediately that he did so, Milo stood up and as James walked to the back door he walked at his side, long tail describing an arc through the air.

"Fickle so and so," James grizzled as they approached the door.

Melissa smiled as she watched them go out into the garden. She spent a moment with her thoughts as they wandered around the edge of the lawn, Milo sniffing everything and anything as he went, this new landscape he was encountering for the first time was filled with interesting scents and smells. The walk around the garden was leisurely and stilted as snuffling was the order of the day. Occasionally, he picked up a rear leg and added to the scentscape.

Melissa joined them, slipping an arm through James, "thank you," she whispered and she kissed his cheek to emphasise her thanks.

Then she stopped.

"What?" asked James as he was drawn to a halt by the anchor of her arm, "everything OK?"

"Fine," she said, "can you take a photo of me and Milo? For the wall?"

James nodded, pulling his phone from his pocket, "I can print it out and stick it up later today."

Melissa was already crouching by Milo and stroking his head. This stroking created a problem. Milo's attention was on Melissa and this was not going to make for a great photo. It could be a photo of a great many dogs, what with it being of a dog's body and the back of its head.

There ensued a protracted series of attempts to capture an

11

image of Milo. Several false dawns were presented to James. Milo would actually present a striking portrait pose that, had James been quick enough with the camera would have made for a tremendous photo. He came close to getting a half decent photo, only to review what was either a blurred image or yet another photo of the back of the dog's head.

James groaned, "never work with children or animals!"

"You're not a film director, dear!" giggled Melissa, she was enjoying the failed photo panto immensely.

James gave Melissa *a look,* "why don't you hold his head?" he suggested.

"Hold a big old dog's head so you can get a photo of him? How do you think that is going to work?!" Melissa rolled her eyes.

"OK clever clogs, what do you suggest?!" James followed this up with a harrumph.

"Have you got something he really likes?" asked Melissa.

"Hold on," said James and he went back inside.

He returned moments later with his left hand enclosing an item of interest to Milo. James readied his camera with his right hand, lowered down on his haunches and when he was good and ready he presented his left hand and opened it to reveal a big dog treat.

The turn of speed from a sedentary Milo was frighteningly impressive, as was his ability to magic the treat out of existence. In his surprise at Milo's antics, James fell backwards on the lawn.

He looked skyward and groaned, his view of the sky was interrupted by his wife, "well? Did you get a photo of the both of us?"

James rolled his eyes.

If he thought things couldn't get worse, he was wrong. Milo interrupted his view of his wife and then affectionately painted his face with dog saliva using a tongue that surely did not fit in that mouth of his. In order to secure a better perch and get a little more comfortable, he climbed on top of the complaining James. For such a chunky dog, he had some deceptively sharp corners and he also knew all about pressure points.

"OOH!" said James

"GERROF!" said James also.

"HELP!" cried the man pinned under a viciously licky dog.

Melissa took pity upon her vanquished husband, "Milo!"

Milo skipped over to his new mistress.

"OW!" cried James as Milo landed a large and heavy poor upon his most delicate region as he propelled himself towards the very nice lady.

James lay there, winded and groaning for a while before unfurling and taking to his feet.

Melissa kissed his cheek, "silly boy!" she chuckled, "here."

She handed him his phone.

"Print that last photo of the two of you, I like that one," she gave James a mischievous look.

He opened his phone and looked down at the screen at his photos. The last photo was of a perfectly posed Milo, tongue lolling and eyes wide and endearing. He was sat still for the camera. On James. This was the photo Melissa wanted.

"Really?" asked James.

"Really," confirmed Melissa.

She linked arms with James again, "You've chosen well, young fella-me-lad. Milo is my first ever dog and I think I might already love him!"

James slipped his arm around his wife and pulled her closer. The movement and the affection were unselfconscious and it was only as he held her that he realised that he didn't want her to see his face right now. Didn't want her to see the emotion that had just come unbidden and threatened to pole-axe him. He hadn't known that Melissa had never had a dog, in fact, he'd always assumed that Melissa and her family had had dogs. They seemed like dog people to him.

That Milo was probably her last ever dog as well as her first, was what had pierced James' heart. He found that he was struggling to breath as he held her against him and it took him what felt like an age to compose himself before he led her and the new man in their lives back inside.

# 12

"Did I get you in trouble when I appeared out of the blue and kept you well beyond your break?" asked James.

They were seated in the same little room and nursing mugs of tea.

"Eh?" Helen was momentarily puzzled, "Oh! No! It wasn't actually my break, I'd clocked off just before you arrived, but that didn't seem to be the right thing to say at the time!"

"Ah!" said James, "you seem pretty good at knowing what to say."

"You have to be," she tilted her head towards the door of the room and the care home beyond.

Of course, to be good at this job, this vocation and life, Helen had to know how to care for the people in this home and a big part of that was knowing how best to act. Maybe it started with the deference and respect that the young should have for their elders and betters, but as that was in short supply, James thought there was a deficit to be made up there in any case. Then there was the disease and fragility that came with it. These people had to be treated the way that archaeologists treated artefacts, with extreme care and forethought, only these were living people and so infinitely more important than that.

Knowing what to say and how to say it was a skill few ever, ever mastered. James had a new found respect for Helen and people like her.

"I hope you don't mind that I came back?" he asked this because suddenly he wondered whether Helen had said it for something reassuring to say. Or that it was a turn of phrase that people said automatically. Things like *see you soon* as part of a goodbye to someone that it was unlikely they would ever see again.

"Do I look like I mind?" admonished Helen.

"No, but..." began James.

"But me no buts and if me no ifs! There aren't that many people who come here because they want to, so I'm certainly not going to turn you away. Besides, I think we had more to talk about didn't we? You'd barely got started. Anyway, I had an ulterior motive..."

James blushed. Oh shit! He'd... was he giving off *signals?* He hadn't meant... this wasn't...

"The dog!" cried Helen, "tell me about the dog and how it went, you fool!!"

The sudden change in subject threw James, but at least it threw him in a direction that he found that he was comfortable with. Milo was Helen's idea, or rather she had heard James say that they could never have a puppy and the idea of Sharemydoggie.co.uk had immediately come to her. James had never heard of the website or the app, but as soon as Helen mentioned it, he knew it was perfect. He'd searched for local dogs and there Milo was. Sometimes things just fell into place, almost like they were meant to be.

"Milo," said James taking a swig of his tea, still not quite over his prior embarrassment.

"Milo, eh? That's one of my favourite ever dogs that," smiled Helen.

"You know Milo?!" James was taken aback.

"No, you numpty! I mean Milo the Jack Russel in The Mask, you know, the Jim Carey film? Milo wears the mask later in the film, but that's not the only reason I love that dog."

"Oh," said James, he'd seen the film years ago, but couldn't recall the dog in question.

"Go on then! What's he like? What breed is he? Did your wife like him!?" Helen was leaning forward now and was all ears.

"He's..." James' brow creased as he tried to work out what Milo actually was, the frown turned to a smile and transformed his face.

"Aw!" Helen patted James' forearm, "You've fallen for him already. How beautiful!"

"No!" protested James.

Helen raised an eyebrow. It was an impressive raising of an eyebrow and not something that would be easily rebutted, but James wasn't going to attempt that anyway.

"I was going to say that Melissa has already fallen for him, but..."

"Yes?"

"Well, the way he came into our home and our lives and the effect he's had... I suppose I've gotta love him for that!"

"So? What is he?!" Helen attempted to chivvy James along, eager to glean what dog had entered his life.

"He's a Basset," replied James.

"Interesting," smiled Helen, "don't they smell funky though?"

"They have a distinctive aroma yes," James found that he was becoming defensive on Milo's behalf.

"And they drool a lot don't they?"

"Only at mealtimes," countered James.

"All worth it though?" asked Helen.

"Yes definitely, he's got these amazing eyes and I swear he can talk. Well almost talk. Very affectionate dog, but not overbearing, unless you happen to be laying on the lawn..."

"Laying on the lawn?" asked a confused Helen.

"Never mind, suffice to say your idea was bang on and as soon as I saw Milo I knew he was the dog for us."

"They don't need much exercise do they?" said Helen, picturing the chunky dogs with small legs.

"Actually, the breed does like long walks, they can go all day. Milo isn't typical of the breed though..."

"Haha! My parents had a dog like that. If you got the lead out she'd sit down and sulk. My Dad had to literally drag and carry her part way around the block. It was only as she got about half way that she started walking and that was only because she knew she was headed back again!"

"That's Milo," agreed James nodding his head.

"So how are things apart from that?" asked Helen.

"Oh, you know. The same," said James.

"No. No they're not," countered Helen.

"Excuse me?" said James, putting his half-drunk mug of tea down.

"Look at you! You're not the same man that walked in off the street a week ago!" smiled Helen.

"Oh... yes... I suppose..."

"You did the right thing. You needed a break and you reached out for help. You needed that," Helen drank some more of her tea.

"Yeah, about that," said James.

"Yes?"

"Can I sit with a resident?"

"Oh! How fickle! Am I not good enough for you now?!" Helen laughed.

James rolled his eyes in response.

Helen gave him an appraising look, then she drew a deep breath, "I'm not going to say no..."

"But?" asked James.

"Well you'll understand that these are my people?"

114

"Yes, of course..."

"No, they're really everything to me. They're family. I've devoted my life to their care and..."

"You want to be careful," said James.

Helen nodded slightly, awkward at the rebuff.

"I understand," and he did, "I walked off the street last week and wasn't even sure how I got here, let alone why."

"There is that," agreed Helen. She was relieved that James was accepting of her reluctance.

"I don't mind waiting," James smiled, "and in the meantime I hope I can still do this?"

"Of course you can!" Helen returned the smile.

"It gives me more time to think. Not that I wouldn't be doing that anyway. I'm not sure I'll be able to explain why I want to sit with the residents. I think it might help."

"It might also not help," sighed Helen.

"How do you mean?" asked James.

"You might be an improvement on when you first came here, but you're obviously in a bad place. You have loads to deal with James, and sitting with reminders of what it is that you have to deal with... well, that could go one of two ways. Besides..."

"Besides?" asked James.

Helen shrugged, uncomfortable, avoiding eye contact.

"Go on, tell me," said James searching for some eye contact in any case.

"Well, you haven't said much about your wife. Don't get me wrong, it might actually be worse if you sat there and gave forth with an endless outpouring..." she pulled a disdainful expression as she said this. She had obviously been cornered and subjected to monologues such as these in the past.

"Are you sure you're cut out for the caring professions?" James asked playfully.

"No. Not sometimes anyway," Helen took a swig of tea, "there's a certain type of person who, when they say 'you're a nurse aren't you?' well, they launch into a litany of woe. There are limits as to how much caring anyone can do and those people sorely test me!"

James laughed. Helen gave him a sharp, warning look, so he tried to explain, "I have friends who wince when people do that to them. One's an accountant and even when he explains that he works in just one area of a wide field, they carry on regardless and won't let up. He's taken to giving them a made up email for them to send their tax queries to. At least he thinks it's made up. Maybe it's real and he's providing a namesake with business!"

Helen smiled, "one of the best ones I heard was one of those types saying 'you're a doctor aren't you?' and without pausing for breath they told this man all about their lopsided man sausage. The doctor in question didn't have the heart to tell him that he was a doctor of philosophy and instead gave him some breathing exercises to do to put his mini leaning Tower of Pisa right!"

"Well, that's one way to deal with it!" exclaimed James.

"Is she on medication?" asked Helen.

The question seemed to stun James. His body responded as though he'd just been sat on by Milo. He sat there for a moment, recovering and composing himself.

"At first, we thought that it might be a tumour. You know, with her age... she's thirty five... Seemed the obvious thing and our GP agreed. Cue lots of tests, and they found nothing."

James shrugged and took a little time again. Helen watched him, careful in her observations, trying to be as gentle as she possibly could.

"It had to be something though, didn't it?" he looked up at her, earnestly and completely laid bare, "the joke wasn't that it's dementia, it's that it's a previously unrecorded and therefore unknown version of dementia. They established this when the inhibitors had no effect..." he laughed bitterly, "...I say that,

Melissa actually had an adverse reaction to them."

"Side effects?"

"No..." James sighed a sigh that wracked his body, "...well, yes. She was pretty ill on them. The worst of it was she had more episodes and if anything, the inhibitors accelerated her dementia."

"Oh, I'm so sorry," Helen's voice almost broke as she said these words.

James looked up and shrugged, he had wanted to thank her and say there was no need to be sorry, but he could neither thank her nor push back her sentiment because he was sorry too.

Helen leant forward, "how long has she got, have they said?"

This question, coming from anyone else, would not have been received well by James, and he was even more raw after his unfortunate encounter with Simon. He was not in total denial, but the one thing he could not bear to look towards was the end. His wife's end. Her mortality was a cruel blow, as was the nature of it and then there was the time that was left to her, some of which would not be life, not a pleasant one anyway. At the end, she would be surviving, if you could even call it that.

"They don't know," James breathed the words out as much as said them.

Helen knew better than to venture her own estimation of Melissa's prognosis. The usual length of time left to older people was eight to ten years. The key words though were *it depends.* Mostly it depended on when dementia had been diagnosed, rolling back from a midpoint to establish how long someone had had dementia was tricky and she knew it was even more difficult in someone so young. Younger people were more active and had a set of well-developed coping strategies for life in general, so they took the early symptoms largely in their stride and just carried on as normal. By the time they, or those around them, realised that something wasn't normal they were a fair way down the track.

It also depended on what form of dementia someone had, that was a bit like cancer. Some cancers weren't all that much of a problem. They weren't pleasant and they necessitated treatment, but they could be dealt with. Others were horrible, angry bastards and by the time they were detected there was nothing that could be done and worse still there was very little time left to the sufferer. Helen also thought that it depended on the person, it wasn't compatibility exactly, but sometimes a disease found a person and unfortunately they got on like house on fire. That wasn't anything to do with strength and how determined someone was to fight – in the face of certain factors just clicking into place there was nothing anyone could do.

Life wasn't fair. It didn't follow a set of knowable rules. There was a chaos to these things that undid all the best efforts of everyone however good they were.

Helen watched James as he considered the time left to his wife. He was diminished somehow. Bent over in his seat and turned inwards. He said something very quietly. The words were so quiet that they took their time to travel through Helen. She registered their sound, but there was a delay in her receiving a meaning.

*She has less than a year.*

That was what he had just said.

Helen's chest hurt. To discover that you or your nearest and dearest had dementia was a terrible thing to bear. The disease was an awful thief. It stole you away, piece by piece. To find that it had come for you early? Half a life time earlier than it was ever due?

Then there was the punchline.

Instead of having the best part of twenty years left, granted they would be difficult years, but many of them would be good. Instead of making it at least to your sixtieth birthday, you were being fast tracked to the end. A frightening, high speed journey through a godawful disease and you'd be lucky to see another birthday and another Christmas.

They sat quietly together for some while. There was nothing left for either of them to say, this particular conversation had come to a natural end.

Eventually, James looked up to find Helen was watching him. He realised that she'd been sat there quietly watching him for a while now.

120

"Fancy watching a spot of TV?" she asked him.

He looked askance at her.

"The TV in the lounge. We can have a sit in there for a little while, if you'd like?"

James didn't challenge her, he resisted returning to her earlier temporary *no*. He got that this was a gentle offer. A small trial. He smiled as he felt a familiar feeling that elicited a memory. As they got up and left the office and walked to the lounge he relived the first ever time he'd gone to visit Melissa's parents. The anticipation and nerves that didn't dissipate as he sat in their living room and watched TV with them. Her father taciturn. Her mother trying for conversation with sporadic conversation, but the ritual of quiet telly watching prevailing so they all sat there and focused on the screen.

"It's usually something like Murder She Wrote, I'm afraid," said Helen as they got to the door of the lounge.

James covered his mouth and suppressed his laughter.

Helen raised that eyebrow of hers.

"Sorry, just had a flashback," he waved away any further questions.

It had been Murder She Wrote when he'd gone to see Melissa's parents that first time.

# 13

J ames had been upstairs putting away the clean laundry and as with many jobs, this spawned other, related jobs that he thought he may as well do as he was there, it would only annoy him if he were to leave those jobs until later, so he ploughed on.

Keeping the house tidy was getting to be more of a challenge. James had to be discrete with some of his tidying because he didn't want Melissa to clock what it was that he was removing and taking to its more natural place. Sometime, he nearly forgot and wanted to make a joke of it, or out of genuine curiosity to ask Melissa why the TV remote was on the toilet cistern and not the toilet in the downstairs cloakroom, no, the remote had travelled upstairs to the bathroom from the arm of the chair in the living room..

Under normal circumstances, yes he would have said something, and most likely added a light-hearted jibe about her losing her marbles. That joke wasn't funny anymore, quite the opposite, and it had lost all of its appeal. It belonged to another James who had lived a long time ago in another place entirely.

James didn't mind picking up after his wife, he hardly thought about it really, he just bimbled around the house putting things away. When he did this, it wasn't the chore he was thinking about anyway. Instead he had a low, almost constant buzz of thoughts concerning Melissa's illness. Those thoughts were like background radiation and James knew that the leak was getting bigger and the radiation would become more powerful and it would eventually kill Melissa. He would survive, but he knew the radiation was taking its toll. He fought to think about other things and focus on things they could do that would provide a welcome distraction for them both, and to an extent he was successful with this, but the radiation was ever present, however much he learnt to ignore it, it was always, always there.

He was picking up discarded clothes from their bedroom floor. Once upon a time the safe assumption would be that these clothes were for the wash basket, that they had been worn at least once. He thought back to when their relationship was fresh and new and they had done that thing that young couples do...

...had they christened every room in the end? Surely not every room. All the major rooms that counted as rooms as far as estate agents were concerned, maybe. That was pretty good going, thought James. He had had partially indiscrete conversations over drinks with the boys and discovered that some relationships were a little more staid and most, if not all the action had occurred in the bedroom. Looking at the clothes strewn over the floor, James recalled the times when they had been in such a rush to get upstairs and enjoy themselves, they had left a trail of discarded clothes on their way up to the bedroom. The extent of today's clothes haul suggested some fun TV show related game where the contestant had to wear as many of the clothes in their wardrobe in a five minute limit as they possibly could. The audience would then decide whether the contestant was a good egg, if so then they would win the holiday in Corfu.

There weren't just clothes on the floor. The inexplicable migration of objects around the house was ramping up. James placed ornaments from downstairs to one side. He'd put them in a carrier bag and find a moment to return them to their rightful place later. Some of the clothes he was picking up were also his, he laughed quietly at a joke he came up with, which was a variation on a theme; *it's alright for her to migrate his clothes when she has dementia, bet it wouldn't be OK if the boot was on the other foot!* He knew it wasn't the most tasteful of jokes, but he'd take his laughs wherever he could get them these days.

As he returned his socks to their drawer he found something sitting in the remaining, un-redistributed socks. A shoe box that he had never seen before. He placed his errant socks on the bed and lifted the lid of the newly discovered box.

He'd expected photos and perhaps a few keepsakes. Part of him felt bad about breaching a code of trust. Betraying his wife's privacy. This part of him was overridden by a curiosity born of the disease that was ravaging his wife. He wanted, no, he needed to know as much of his wife as he could before there was nothing left to know. He was on the clock and there would never be enough time. Bit by bit, parts of his wife were being

13

snatched from them both. Besides, some of what was in this box could go on the memory wall. Photos of a younger version of Melissa. A fresh faced Melissa with an embarrassing hair cut that she'd picked on her way to finding what best suited her, this paired with some fashion blunders too. Everyone had those sorts of photos, it was a part of growing up.

James sometimes wished that they had met earlier. He assumed that they would have got together whenever they had met, and to know her when she was younger would have been great. He loved his wife, and what could be better than spending their youth together? He'd had these thoughts soon after they had gotten together – the delight in seeing her as a girl and being there with her as they grew up. Now he kept them at bay for fear they would hurt too much.

James was right about the contents of the box, he was also completely off the mark. As he lifted the lid he saw photos and upon seeing them he felt his anticipation lift to excitement. Then he realised what it was that he was looking at and the excitement crashed and was replaced with a dizzy numbness.

The photo on top was black and white and nothing like anything James was expecting to see. The image was alien, and yet it was completely familiar. James knew what it was the instant it was revealed. He also knew what it *meant.* There was no escaping what it was that he was looking at and it's meaning. James stood there for what felt like a long while, it was only a matter of seconds, but this moment signified a change in his life and there was no going back from this. Even if he closed the box, he could never forget what he had seen.

125

He lifted the box carefully and almost ceremoniously and oblivious to the socks laying on the bed, he sat down upon them and placed the box on his lap. He lifted the photo of the scan of a baby growing inside a woman and stared at it. He knew that the woman this baby had grown in was Melissa.

He placed the scan next to him on the bed and looked down at the box. He had to know, knew it was better to know now that he'd opened the box. That leaving his mind to fill in the details would be a form of torture. Despite this, he was cautious as he returned to the box. He paused and took a deep breath. There were more photos and under the photos the unmistakeable edges of envelopes which undoubtedly contained letters.

James knew what he was going to find, or at least he knew the outline of what it was. His examination of the contents of the box would partially fill that outline. Then it was a case of...

...of what?

Would he ask Melissa about this?

Could he ask her?

How would he broach the subject? Even before she had fallen ill. How would he do that now though? Everything had changed.

Better to know now he had gone this far and opened the box though. Better now than...

He couldn't bear to think about that and instead he found he was holding a pile of photos of Melissa with a broad and angular young man. He shuffled through the photos, looking at one after another, putting each one to the back in order to view the next. He had gone through the pile at least twice before he realised that he couldn't remember where he had started and which photo had been at the top of the pile.

He laughed. The laugh caught him by surprise, as did the tears through which he was laughing. The cause of his laughter was a cruel thought; *as if she will know I've been snooping. As if she'll remember the order the photos had been left in.*

James sobbed. His tears were the tears of loss and a strange jealousy. He would never again have what he could see in the photos. Not now. He had had it once and he'd had the very best of Melissa and that was all that counted, but the emotions that memories evoke are inexplicable at the best of times. James knew that underlying all of this there was happiness, that he was thinking of the times he had had with Melissa as he filed through the images before him.

He put the photos to one side, next to the scan. He lifted the first of the envelopes, turned it and saw the letters SWALK. Young love. It was almost compulsory to seal love letters with a kiss. He thought that, were he to raise the envelope to his nose there would be the hint of an aftershave popular at the time and somewhere there was another, corresponding shoe box with a pile of letters that smelt of Melissa's perfume. Thinking this, he withdrew the envelope and he read.

The letter was the letter of a love struck teenager. The words could almost have been his when he was that age. They took him back to a time that only in retrospect could he say was carefree. At the time there had been such intensity and angst and he wondered whether, with age, he had become cynical. Love's young dream wasn't real and it couldn't last.

In this case, James knew the ending. It hadn't lasted. There was the matter of that scan though. The scan spoke of a beginning and a whole other path on Melissa's journey through life that James was oblivious to.

He came to the end of the first letter, it was signed by Dmitri. James looked down at the pile of photos and at the man, or rather the boy who would be a man. He was called Dmitri. That made a kind of sense. The name fit with the images. It was an unusual name though and this interested James. It was yet another hook to draw him in. How was Dmitri different to him and why had Melissa chosen first Dmitri and then James?

Carefully returning the letter to the envelope, James considered the pile of letters. He wanted to pluck the letter from the very bottom. He guessed that was the letter that would tell him what had happened and how things had ended. Would that letter be the letter where Dmitri ended things with Melissa, telling her that they were too young to have a child, that he had spoken with his parents and they had forbidden he see her again.

Did Dmitri know about their child?

Was the final letter a desperate plea to Melissa to reconsider.

To take him back and try again. This time, things would be different. Would that letter even tell James how things had ended, after all, these were only one side of the correspondence and there was no telling what was in Melissa's letters.

A sound.

Footsteps on the stairs.

"Shit!" James hissed under his breath.

He dropped the letters back in the box and grabbed at the photos and then the scan. He hurriedly slapped the lip back on the box and go to his feet. He eyed the open sock draw, but that didn't seem to be the right place to put the box. It felt odd and out of kilter, which was exactly what it was. His eyes raced around the room looking for a place he could stash the box. He needed a place where, if Melissa were to find it, would make a kind of sense to her and the largest part of that sense he wanted to convey was that James hadn't seen it.

He strode around to her side of the bed and quickly got to his hands and knees and slipped the box under Melissa's side of the bed, breathing out a sigh of relief as it fit beneath with no dramas.

"James?"

Melissa was in the room.

James straightened and looked over at his wife in the door way.

"What are you doing?" she asked him as he emerged from by the bed.

"Just a spot of tidying," he said raising his hand and waggling what he thought was a pair of his socks to demonstrate the task he was currently undertaking. For good measure, he threw the would-be socks onto the pile he'd left on the bed.

"A tea towel?" asked Melissa.

James looked at what he had just thrown onto the bed, and upon seeing a scrunched up tea towel, fought back a frown before it developed on his forehead, "I was doing a spot of dusting too."

"With a tea towel?"

"Yeah, it's bigger than a dust cloth. Dunno why more people don't use them for dusting," he shrugged. The shrug was as much at himself and how easily he had entered into this fabrication. He didn't have a clue where it had come from, but he had to avoid upsetting Melissa at all costs.

"And you were dusting the floor on my side of the bed?" Melissa wasn't quite buying James story.

"Oh no, I picked up a couple of things from this side of the bed and then realised that I must've dropped my giant dust cloth," James smiled, then regretted the smile. The smile was probably too much.

"OK," Melissa's brow knotted.

James didn't think that she was convinced, but he hoped that she just thought that he had a novel approach to household chores. He'd been caught between a rock and a hard place because he was also reluctant to admit he'd been collecting items from the floor for fear that she might connect this with what James sometimes called her absences. The moments when she was no longer there and was unaware of her own actions. He didn't want to add to her discomfort or confusion, but knew he had. Hopefully this was a different confusion and aimed entirely at him.

She looked at the bed and then James again, "I'm feeling done in, do you mind if I take a nap?"

James stood up, "not at all, I'll just finish putting my socks away."

Melissa's eyes flicked towards the socks on the bed and the open drawer, "you'll have to do something else before you do that."

James tried to steady his voice, he felt like a naughty school boy and was still terrified that he was going to be busted, "What's that then?"

"Come here and give me a hug?" she said it meekly and uncertainly.

James went to her straightaway and wrapped his arms around

her, holding her tight. They stayed like that for quite a while, then James broke away and led her to the bed, planting a kiss on her forehead even as her eyes were closing.

He closed the curtains before he left and then paused in the doorway to look back at his already slumbering wife. His heart almost burst through his chest, he loved her so much. As he turned to leave the bedroom, his eyes moved away from the sleeping form of his wife and came away via a particular spot in the bedroom. He had a scratch that he really wanted to itch now and he would not leave it too long to discover what else was in those letters.

# 14

That first time with the residents in the lounge, Helen had introduced James to everyone, much the same as a teacher introduces a new pupil to a class. He'd taken an empty seat and found himself watching the TV. There were a few looks exchanged, but that was it as far as excitement was concerned.

James was reminded that, if you were to relax, go with the flow and not to worry so much, a lot of life was unremarkable. It was waiting. It was repetition. It was downtime. It was moving from one thing to another with little recognition of the journey itself. That, if you were not careful, you could wake up one day and realise that a large chunk of your life had passed you by. Then, if you threw in stress, worry and over-thinking? All that did was to waste more precious time and accelerate you through life.

Focus. It was all about focus.

James now understood that he had entered a room that to his badly focused mind, contained dementia sufferers. As he'd sat there and relaxed into his environment though, he instead spent time with people. They were first and foremost, people. If he'd entered a room full of redheads, he'd have been insane to retain a total focus on their redheadedness and what that meant for his time in the room with them. That was clearly wrong, but it didn't stop people doing it. The trick was to know that was what you were likely to do and make the effort to do something about it, at least distract yourself and do something else as a result.

Maybe this was what he'd needed. Why he had asked to sit with the residents. Not to quiz them about their illness like an investigative reporter on a mission, gleaning more knowledge so he could fight alongside Melissa. OK, they said *know thine enemy,* and what James knew after this visit was that dementia was not the be all and end all and that were he to think like that, then he would be allowing it to win and that he was certain to struggle all the more.

As Angela Lansbury brought the episode to a close, tying up the loose ends with only a pedestrian amount of drama, James took this as a cue to leave. He looked at his watch automatically, even though he knew he had to get back.

"Harold!"

The voice was tremulous, excited and loud. James stopped in his tracks. Shocked and stunned, he froze in place. A white haired woman approached him and smiled a huge smile. A smile that James knew that he did not deserve. A smile that was not for him, but for someone else. A someone else who no longer existed other than in this woman's mind's eye.

"Harold! Where have you been!? I've been looking for you everywhere! Come with me!"

She turned and started walking away, out of the lounge through a door that James had not been through before. She turned, sensing quite rightly that James, or rather Harold, was not following her.

"Come on! What are you waiting for!?" she waved a beckoning hand.

James broke out of his stupor and caught her up, sensing that any protest, let alone an attempt to put the woman straight, would be unkind and maybe damaging. At the very least, it would be upsetting and James didn't want to upset anyone if he could help it.

Before he could go through the door and exit the lounge however, another woman with an obligatory blue rinse urgently beckon him over. Curious, he did as he was bade.

"Here, take this. I've always wanted you to have it," she smiled kindly as she pushed an object into his palm and closed his fingers around it.

"Harold! What are you doing with that woman! You said you'd changed! I knew you couldn't be trusted!"

The white haired was stood in the doorway and very angry. James scampered towards her, "Sorry, I was..."

"I know what you were doing and I won't have it, do you hear?!" she gave him a very stern look, "now come on, and no more delays!"

James followed her and as she turned right into a room, he realised she had led him back to her own room. As he rounded the door he was greeted with the sight of her sitting on the bed and pulling her nightdress to one side to expose a shoulder.

"At long last, we're alone. It's been so long Harold. Quick, shut the door!"

James stood agog. His mouth hanging open. He certainly hadn't been expecting this and his capacity to think on his feet was nowhere to be seen, it had taken to its heels when he was greeted with this surprise tableau. All James could think of was where this was headed and how he really didn't want it to go there.

Mustering what thoughts he could, his only coherent strategy was to protest and that protest consisted of denying that he was Harold. He didn't think for one moment that this would work, worse still, he expected it to end badly and embarking on such a course of action was therefore tantamount to cruelty. He was the responsible party here and he had to make good this situation. The longer he delayed, the worse the outcome. Doing nothing was the worst of the options available to him.

"I have to go and powder my nose!" he blurted.

"Powder your nose?" the woman on the bed looked uncertain,

"you've never said those words in your life, Harold. Are you having a funny turn?" she scrutinised James.

James wondered what it was that she was seeing. He didn't want the façade to tumble down for her and for that to lead to hurt and confusion.

"I'm going to the bathroom and I will be right back," he said this with more confidence. He was telling her. He was attempting to be manly and do things with gusto.

There was no rebuttal, so he nodded and quickly turned on his heel, going back the way he came. He exited the lounge the way he had originally come and almost bumped into Helen in his rush to find her.

"What's up?" she asked. She was looking him up and down as though to establish where he was injured.

"You've got to come quickly!" he realised that he was out of breath and struggling to get the words out.

"Calm down," Helen placed a hand on his forearm and led him back into the office where they'd drunk their tea earlier.

Once the door was shut she turned to him, "so what happened?"

"Well I watched the TV and everything was fine until I got up to leave and then I was accosted by a woman who thought I was Harold..."

Helen nodded, "Ah, that'll be Connie," she smiled, "took you to her bedroom did she?"

"Yes! And she... well, I think Harold was her husband or something because..."

"She showed you a bit of shoulder didn't she?"

"Yes... how did you?"

"Harold was her sweetheart during the war. I don't think they ever went beyond first base. They pledged their undying love to each other and then off he went to fight and he never came back."

"Oh..." James felt the wind fall from his sails, "...how sad."

"Some memories are, aren't they? But we'd not be without them would we? I mean, it may be sad on the face of it, but was she sad just now?"

"No, far from it!"

"There you go then," Helen frowned, "you didn't tell her you weren't Harold did you? Or argue with her?"

"No. I did my best not to contradict her or upset her. I... told her I needed the bathroom..."

"Good. You did good."

14

James expelled a deep breath of air. Something about being told he had done good by Helen was a relief, he felt more relaxed and in feeling more relaxed he realised how keyed up he had been.

"What's that in your hand?" enquired Helen.

In all the mad excitement, James had forgotten he had anything in his hand. He lifted his closed hand and revealed the object to them both. It was a small troll doll with a shock of bright green hair.

Helen took it gently from him, "that's Dot's. She regularly hands it out to people, but if it's not in her room later, she'll not be happy!"

"Oh," said James, "you have a lot going on here don't you?"

Helen eyed him appraisingly, "I told you, they're my people and I care about them. They're no different to anyone else. You get to know the people you care about and you learn what works and what definitely doesn't."

She shrugged, James thought it was a self-deprecating shrug, a *you-just-do-it-don't-you?* kind of shrug.

"I think you underestimate just how much work you're putting in here," said James, he was now leaning back against the door.

"It's not work if you enjoy what you're doing," she countered, "the work bit is all the lifting and sorting and cleaning. I have muscles I never knew I had!"

She caught James looking at her arms.

He shook his head as though waking up from a day dream, "I'm sorry, I seem to be on the back foot half the time and not quite with it. It's exhausting."

"Yes. Yes, it is. Especially to begin with. You've a lot to learn. It gets easier with practice though."

James shrugged, he supposed it did, his problem was that he was still fighting it and he didn't want to practice. He was way off acceptance and wasn't sure he could ever accept the hand he and Melissa had been dealt by life.

"I'd better go, the lady who comes to spend time with Melissa and do a spot of cleaning and tidying will be heading off soon." He pushed himself from the door and grasped the handle.

"You'll be back though, will you?" Helen's voice was neutral, matter-of-fact.

"Yes," James smiled, "if you'll have me?"

"Course we will," Helen raised an eyebrow, "Connie and Dot haven't put you off then?"

James wanted to give an instant no. They hadn't, but that single word didn't seem like the truth of it. He hadn't been put off, not really, but...

14

He raised a hand, keeping it flat and horizontal, he waved it up and down to signify *so-so,* "If I'm honest, and I think I really have to be honest. With myself I really do... yeah, I was put off. If I didn't need to be here, then I think I could well have run and never turned back," he sighed, but maintained eye contact with Helen, "that makes me sound weak, doesn't it?"

"Yup," she said it casually, but it felt heavy. Weighed down with more meaning than the simple word itself should be capable of containing.

James waited, but no further words were forthcoming, "Oh. Right. Well, thanks for your support there... I..."

"Get over yourself, James!" there was laughter tinging her words now, "don't be so hard on yourself. Of course you're weak. You have to work at this in order to get stronger. There are no shortcuts and this isn't easy. What in life is? The worthwhile stuff anyway!"

James saw the wisdom in her words, but he still felt like a bit of a loser, "I should have done better..."

"Right, listen to me," Helen's voice had become firm and business-like and for the first time, James saw that she was not to be trifled with. He thought he'd known that anyway, but now he could see it right before his eyes, "you don't need to be here. You chose to come here and right now, you're still here. I'd say that is a result. Also a result is that you had the strength to be honest just now. You opened up and described what had happened. If you're doing that then you are dealing with the situation and that in my book is all good. OK?"

James nodded.

"OK?!" she almost shouted it now.

"Yes OK," James said immediately and his voice had taken on an edge of protest, to his own ears he sounded a bit teenagery.

Helen flinched at his words, or rather the way he had said them, she softened, "Sorry, it's just... I suppose yours is a perfectly natural reaction and I've seen it many times over the years, only you are doing something about it. If I had a pound for every time I saw someone reacting the way you have, but not doing anything about it, not putting the work in... *not coming back.*"

They shared a quiet moment, then Helen cleared her throat, "and they need to come back. It's their mum or their dad, but they choose themselves instead. They can't bear to put the effort in and instead they remain weak. These people gave them *life!* They put in the work! And that's before you even look at this generation! They went through hell for us and we don't know the half of it! The stories James! The things these people can tell us and we run the risk of losing out on all of it if we just give up and stay weak..."

James made a concerted effort not to let his jaw drop for a second time that day. He also did his best not to stare, which was a problem as his eyes went all over the place and made him feel uncomfortable. This sudden display of passion was awesome. Helen was transformed right before him. That was strength alright and that was also caring.

"Sorry..." she whispered, "I just get so..."

"Don't be..." James cut in, "you have every right... and I'm glad you just said that."

"You are?" there was surprise in her words.

"Yes!" he exclaimed, "If I was ever in need of a pep talk, it's now and that was it."

"Oh, I..." began Helen.

"You did good, and you reminded me of what counts, thank you."

James patted Helen's forearm. This wasn't a usual gesture for him, but it was unselfconscious and felt right, "Thank you," he said again nodding for emphasis.

Then he was opening the door and passing through it.

He stopped in the open doorway and turned, "same time next week?"

Helen nodded and smiled.

As James left, he realised he'd seen tears in her eyes.

# 15

Awake.

The strange disorientation that accompanies an unexpected awakening. Strobing through reality and dream-state, a sick feeling in his gut. James isn't sure why he's awake, only that it's dark, he's dog tired and he shouldn't be awake. The pull towards slumber, the urge to roll over and return to sleep is strong.

He can't.

There's something wrong.

That feeling of wrongness comes crashing through now and suddenly he's sat bolt upright. Listening carefully at something in the dark. When the sound does not come, he turns to look down beside him, his eyes only now adjusting to the darkness and he senses more than sees what it is that has awoken him.

An absence.

Melissa is not there in the bed beside him.

Then he hears it.

A gentle, plaintive cry.

He pivots on his butt, his feet finding the floor. He takes a moment to rub the sleep from his eyes, then he stands, automatically grabs his lounge pants and clambers into them, his foot catching in the right leg and almost causing him to overbalance and pitch forwards. He grumbles something indecipherable at himself for his sleepy awkwardness.

As he leaves the bedroom, he hopes against hope that Milo was unsettled and Melissa crept down to let him out then give him a fuss until he'd lain still. The alternatives are scrolling through his mind and the sick feeling caused by a rude awakening is amplified as he heads downstairs.

The sound of the distressed dog is louder as he nears the foot of the stairs. He is walking carefully as he makes his way down the stairs and through to the kitchen, he has to be careful as the house remains in darkness and without thinking, he knows that it's a bad idea to turn the lights on, that flicking any of the switches may cause Melissa an unnecessary shock to her already beleaguered system.

James knows something is wrong, knew from the moment he awoke. What adds to his concern is that Melissa has never been quiet when it comes to navigating her away around or out of the bedroom. Something in the way Melissa is built means that she always makes more noise and fuss and disruption than is ever necessary. Many is the time that Melissa has woken James only for her to roll over and fall straight to sleep, leaving him staring at the ceiling wondering when his visit to slumberland will happen, if ever. That she has slipped from their marital bed like a ghost and for the first time in their shared life, managed not to wake him, concerns him greatly.

The kitchen is in absolute darkness. Before they turned in last night, they closed the blinds to ensure Milo would sleep through. They didn't want him howling them awake at the crack of dawn. Carefully, James opens the kitchen blinds until he can see via the night-blue light.

Melissa is sitting motionless at the dining room table, her laptop open in front of her. There is no light emanating from the screen and James wonders how long she has sat like that for the laptop to lapse into sleep mode.

Right now Milo is giving forth sad, whining moans and the sound of him damn near breaks James' heart, he doesn't think he's ever heard a dog sound so sad and forlorn. He kneels near the form of the sitting dog and as he reaches out to stroke and reassure him, he sees that he has his head on Melissa's lap and he's staring up at her with pleading eyes. Even in the ethereal night, Milo's eyes are visible, large and shining. James is thankful for the dog and the way he has bonded with Melissa. Milo has been looking out for her and gently calling for James until he came to help out.

James whispers to Milo, "C'mere, mate."

15

Milo takes a final, lingering look at Melissa and then pads reluctantly to James. who makes a fuss of him and gets him to lay on his bed. James notes that Milo can't take his eyes off Melissa. He won't take his eyes of Melissa, he's looking out for one of his own.

James gently takes Melissa's elbow and guides her upwards, managing to shift her chair with his leg to make more room for her as she rises. She makes no sound as helps her to her feet and she comes with him with no resistance. He feels like he's guiding a sleep walker carefully to bed and in a way, he supposes that he is.

He gets her back to their bed with no dramas, her motor memory helping her to find her way back as much as James is. She slips back into bed and sighs. He watches her for a long while, not daring to hope that she truly is asleep and the night's drama is over.

His vigil is disturbed by a groaning sigh. He looks down to find Milo laying at Melissa's bedside, his head resting on his front legs and eyes firmly on his mistress. James hadn't noticed Milo slink along behind them. One of the only firm house rules for Milo was that he wasn't to come upstairs. Under the circumstances, Milo has made exactly the right call. James is glad he is here, sitting guard over Melissa.

"I'll get your bed mate," he whispers to the dog.

Milo doesn't look away from Melissa, but his tale wags once in response; *OK.*

147

James carefully creeps out of the bedroom. He gets all the way to the kitchen without turning the lights on. He doesn't want to break the spell of the night. He glances down at Milo's bed before walking to the sink, grabbing a glass from the nearby overhead cupboard and filling it at the tap. He downs the contents of the glass as he stares out into the nothingness of the night. He lets out a long breath before returning to the other side of the kitchen and sitting at the dining table.

This is the real reason he is here. He has to know why Melissa came down here in the early hours and fired up her laptop. Why she was sat here in the dark, her eyes unseeing. He barely registers his activities as snooping, a potential breach of trust. There are more important factors at play here now and James' role is moving away from his previous role as partner and towards one of guardian, protector and carer. The real truth of it is that he is now both. He has to juggle the two roles and make them work because he is still Melissa's husband and her life partner and this has to be a constant. She needs this and she needs him in this capacity. His other role is a counter to her disease, it is his natural response to the *other* her. The side to her that she does not and cannot fully see.

He swipes the mouse pad and the laptop lights up. There is a momentary transition from the wallpaper to the screen that Melissa was viewing, then there is a delay between the screen appearing and James registering what it is that he is seeing.

He gasps and his hand unselfconsciously finds itself at his mouth, covering it.

Oh no, he thinks, and the two words loop around and around as he takes in what he is looking at.

Melissa had been looking up dementia on the internet. There is some received wisdom on this subject and it runs along the lines of *never do an internet search of your symptoms, the results that come up on the search will damn near kill you with stress.* The hits for a search on symptoms are always the worst cases. Lots and lots of worse cases.

In some ways, the results of Melissa's search and the article that she was reading at the kitchen table, bucks this trend. There aren't multifarious, bleak and terrible ways to die from her condition, there is just the inexorable march towards a state of affairs where forgetting ends a life. The disease grows and grows and as it does, confusion and forgetting are the order of the day.

Melissa was reading about how she would die. James guesses, quite rightly as it happens, that she searched using words that asked...

*How do you die of dementia*

...the answer to this is that quite simply, your body forgets how it functions. You struggle to eat, food remaining forgotten in your mouth, but it is not starvation or dehydration that is likely to kill you, although they will be creeping up on you and wasting you away, no you will choke and asphyxiate as the dementia confuses your most basic of motor functions and you no longer know how to breath properly. Dementia will lean over you and close its cold fingers around your throat and strangle you to death.

James is breathing heavily and fighting waves of emotion. Wanting to take this away. At least take away the dark knowledge that Melissa now harbours. She shouldn't know about this terrible eventuality. The spectre of this knowing hanging over them both and marring the remaining days that they have together. But it is too late. She knows. James knows. There is no happy ending here.

James shuts the laptop down.

A dialogue pops up asking if he wants the forced shut down of…

He taps yes, just wanting that screen to go away.

He hasn't noticed that the internet screen he was viewing was just one of many, that Melissa had opened page after page of information concerning dementia. That she had gone on that journey that people sometimes do of clicking links and spiralling away from the initial line of enquiry to first one tangent and then another and then another. There was a logic to Melissa's searching though, and a conclusion.

James closed the lid of the laptop, leaving it where it was. Satisfied that it was now off and clear of that screen. He got up and stooped to pick up Milo's bed before heading back up to bed. Doubting that he would get any sleep after what he had seen.

Absently he dropped Milo's soft bed at the side of Melissa's bed. There was no dog there though. He looked around the room, wondering where Milo had got to, his eyes finally resting on his spot on the bed. Milo was sprawled crossways on James side of the bed, his head on Melissa's lap.

"Dog!" James whispered, marvelling at the humour in his own voice.

The humour increased as Milo opened one eye a flicker to observe him then lowered his droopy eyelid again, feigning constant slumber.

James padded around the bed and removed his lounge pants. Moving Milo around so he could actually get into bed was easier said than done, the dog providing him with something beyond a dead weight. In the end, Melissa stirred and this had the effect of shifting Milo around a little. James slipped into the space afforded to him. He lay there balancing precariously on the edge of the bed, wondering whether he should use the spare room instead, but not wanting to leave Melissa. Milo took pity on him and moved around so he was between the two of them. James stroked behind his ear by way of thanks and Milo gave a contented sigh before drifting quickly off to sleep, James watched him, envious of the ease with which he could enter a sleep state.

He continued stroking the dog and this was probably what helped eventually take him from his wakeful state...

# 16

When James awoke, the day was already underway. The curtains were still drawn, but from the quality of light streaming around the curtain edges, he could see that it was well into the morning. He looked to his right. No Melissa.

Then he remembered the third occupant of the bed. No sign of him either.

Sounds drifted up from downstairs and on the heels of those sounds the unmistakeable aroma of bacon.

He quickly got up and got ready, showering in a matter of minutes and throwing on some clothes.

"Hello sleep head, you're just in time!" Melissa greeted him as he entered the kitchen, "what's that you've got there?"

"Notepad and pen," he raised them both to show her more clearly.

"And you have them because...?"

"Because after that tasty breakfast," he nodded towards the two plates and noticed Milo sat patiently, his total focus now on both Melissa *and* the two plates of food. The aromas floating down from them must be torture for the poor lad, thought James, "I'm going to start taking notes as you tell me all about the favourite times in your life."

"You're serious about writing my autobiography then?" she'd cocked her head to one side, better to read him with.

"It's not going to be your autobiography... more a record of your life... and something for us to share," he shrugged.

Melissa took pity on him and smiled, "it's all a bit weird isn't it?"

She turned away from him before anything else could be said and took up the two plates, he watched her placing them at the table, then he slipped his arms around her before she could move away from his place setting and returned to her own to take a seat.

"What's weird is that people fail to do this. They drift through their lives and they fail to talk. Not properly anyway. I bet there's people in pubs that know more about each other than their own families do. We can all miss so much if we're not careful."

He gave her a squeeze in his arms and she looked up at him, "and you want to be careful?"

He nodded, "I've never thought about that word in that context before, *careful* is usually a bit of a boring word isn't it? But full of care? Actually taking time to care? Yeah. We have this time, so let's use some of it like this, eh? You down with that?"

Melissa nodded and grinned, breaking his grip on her, "but first, breakfast!"

* * *

Breakfast went down a treat, James didn't realise how hungry he was and the food revitalised him after the night of disturbed sleep he had had. He cleared the plates, knives and forks and returned to the table to conduct the business of the day. Placing the writing pad deliberately before him, he took up his pen. Melissa cleared her throat and shifted in her chair composing herself, then she reached across the table and pulled the pad to her, she gestured with her hand for James to hand over his pen. He did so meekly, looking askance of his wife.

"Go on then!" she chuckled.

James was confused, this was not in the script. Not in his script anyway. Melissa had turned the tables on him.

Melissa gave James a certain look, it was the kind of look an adult gives a child and can mean a whole range of things, but here it meant *you didn't really think you'd get away with this did you?*

154

"You first, James. I don't live in a vacuum and my story won't make sense without you in it, will it?"

James got that she was right, but he didn't want to waste time, "But I..." he began.

"Sharing, James. This is all about sharing, so I want to hear your stories too, OK?"

And that was that. James couldn't argue with her logic. If he were to hear her stories then he had to give of himself too. He had to tell her his stories. That should make for a dialogue, encouraging them both to talk and more importantly, to open up. To inspire each other and push each other towards times and stories they may well have overlooked under any other circumstances.

Where to start?

James began at the beginning with his earliest memories. These were not necessarily coherent and he wondered how much of his fall from his bicycle was rehearsed and infilled by his Mother via many retellings of the story. He told Melissa about the recurring dream he had after the fall. Sitting at the top of the stairs in the first house they had lived in, or at least he thought it was, he couldn't remember much of the interior, the exterior he did remember, the sandpit that he'd buried his indestructible Tonka toys in, rendering them malleable and all too destructible after a winter in the ground. The drive way that he'd driven his green pedal car, Lotus up and down on. Eventually becoming bored of the restricted circuit and driving into the wall of the house repeatedly until the front end was shattered and he could see the pedals and his feet on them, the number seven sticker on the nose cone now sagging under the weight of a piece of the car that was trying to hang on for dear life.

In his dream, he sat at the top of the stairs. Alone. The house was always empty and no one ever came, even as his distress and panic built. The focal point of the dream was his knee and the hole in it. Not the small hole a stone had made when he fell from his bicycle. The site of his small scar was now wide open and much, much bigger. There was no blood and somehow that made the wound all the more frightening.

"Did you ever tell your Mum and Dad about that dream?" Melissa asked him.

James shook his head, "no, I don't think I ever did."

Melissa didn't ask him the why of it. That hung between them in any case.

"Childhood is a strange phase of your life isn't it?"

Melissa nodded. There were things that happened during childhood, ways that you behaved that when you looked back just didn't make sense now. It did back then though. It all made sense. The shame of it was losing touch with that other self. The urge to grow up was destructive. Was that necessary, thought James to himself, did you have to destroy that version of yourself to become the person you were today?

16

"Cup of tea?" James asked.

Melissa nodded, "and then you can get to the important story."

James got up and walked to the kitchen side, fussing over the mugs and tea bags as the kettle boiled, "and what important story would that be?"

He asked this with his back to her, as though he knew the answer already, but didn't want to see it. Didn't want to receive it face on.

"You're going to tell me who it was who broke your heart and how she did it," said Melissa in a matter-of-fact way. This one was apparently not up for negotiation. Not if James wanted her to open up and tell him her stories. This was the price and he would have to pay it.

She watched her husband and saw him stiffen as she landed the request. He tried to relax again, but as he poured the boiling water onto the tea bags he remained stiff and awkward.

"OK," was all that he said.

James held back on the retort that was on his lips, he almost let slip with his own request, but knew it would be wrong and possibly cruel, to confront her with what he had found and demand an explanation. He had to respect her and he wanted her to share her story on her own terms, that was the only way. He took a deep breath. She'd landed an unintentional blow. A blow that surprised him. Some wounds never heeled, they just

157

got covered up and hidden away. Only, she had seen it despite it being covered and hidden. She'd always known. Melissa knew that he was damaged goods and she'd stuck with him and thrown her lot in with him for the long haul anyway.

He stirred the tea bags around and squeezed them against the mug. He liked strong tea.

How had he not seen her wound? He'd not consciously spotted it anyway. And he'd never suspected that she had the past that he had so recently uncovered. He knew his wife less than he'd believed he had. She had more of an inkling of who he was and she'd gone straight to the heart of the matter. Maybe her past experiences had helped her become more adept at this, whereas his hadn't. More to the point, the way she had dealt with things in her past had allowed her to grow. James seemed to have more work to do.

He finished the tea making and placed her mug in front of her, returning to his seat he looked up at her and found that this was more difficult than he could ever have managed. He didn't want to talk about it. He'd closed the door on this part of his life.

"Her name was Tracy and we got together when we were doing A-Levels," he began.

"Tracy?" she wrote this down and drew a heart around it.

James watched her, not sure that he was comfortable with that childish rendering of a heart and the name encased within it.

He went on in any case and he told her the whole story. He figured that starting at the beginning would be easier on him, that bit was the standard script for love's young dream and a story common to most people. As James told it, he realised that he'd been as much playing out a part as anything else. He'd done what he'd been expected to, or what he expected he was supposed to do anyway.

"They fuck you up, your Mum and Dad..." whispered James to himself.

"What was that?" asked Melissa.

James looked up, a dazed look upon his face. He hadn't been aware that he'd spoken.

"I... it's a poem by Philip Larkin, it's called This Be The Verse," explained James.

"A cheerful little ditty then!?" smiled Melissa.

James watched her write it down. He wasn't sure that it was pertinent. Then he winced inwardly. The opening line was all he ever remembered of the poem, that and the sentiment of sin being passed on and added to generation after generation such that the eventual weight of it all would crush humanity. James didn't entirely agree, but he did see inculcated patterns of behaviour that had been observed and adopted by children and unless some serious work was put in, those same illogical and destructive patterns would go on forever. He seemed to remember that the poem was dark and had a suggestion of suicide. It also advised not to have kids yourself in order to break the horrendous, eternal pattern of pain and anguish.

This was not a poem he should have shared with Melissa and he hoped that she wouldn't look it up.

"It's relevance is..." James took a deep breath, "it's a quandary really. Largely, my parents did well in bringing me up. They were very clear on doing things the right way and having respect for others. But they over egged things and they didn't prepare me for some of life's knocks. I don't know how you go about doing that. Telling a child that life is shit, that it is cruel and it will dig its talons into you and pull and tear? It has to be done, or the poor kid walks headlong into a world of pain, but it also doesn't seem right somehow does it? Pointing out how hard life is going to be?"

He looked up at Melissa and winced outwardly this time. He was preaching to the converted. Her expression and her response were inscrutable, but he thought she seemed sad all of a sudden.

"In this particular case," James launched back into it, keen to move the focus back to him and his story, "my parents drummed into me the importance of being kind to the opposite sex. You know, the traditional values of women being the fairer sex and that men should defer to them and treat them right. They overcooked this one though."

"How so?" asked Melissa.

16

"I saw women as something *other*. Especially when it came to that one special and important relationship. My folks made me construct a pedestal on which to put that woman I was destined to meet, and I saw her as a princess and a different species to me. I created something nearing perfection. Something that could do no wrong and this blinded me to the person underneath my construction."

"So when she fell from grace it hurt all the more?" Melissa got it.

"Yeah, it shattered my world, let alone breaking my heart. I didn't expect it. Didn't see it coming and I certainly wasn't equipped to deal with it."

"I think we all do that James," Melissa reached out and took his hand and squeezed it, "at least to a certain extent. We invest ourselves totally that very first time."

James attempted a smile and found it harder than it should have been, "a high risk strategy that works out for some people."

"Does it though?" asked Melissa.

James thought about it, then nodded his head, "you know, I've never trusted the sugar coated couples, the ones who say 'forty years together and never an angry word between us', that's bollocks isn't it? That's not a relationship and at least one of them is having to bend and contort to an unnatural extent. They'll never know each other. Not truly. They'll never grow

161

together."

"So in order to grow, those scales have to fall from your eyes, one way or another..." ventured Melissa.

James nodded.

"So what did she do?" asked Melissa.

"She shagged someone else," replied James.

"Oh, route one eh?"

"Yes. A classic and well told tale. The guy in question was everything I wasn't..."

"That's never good, to have that shadow cast over you," sighed Melissa.

"Too true, but it wasn't that he was bigger and better and someone I would aspire to be, respect and like in other circumstances. No, he was the opposite in a bad way and that hurt all the more. He was smaller and he was an arrogant and smarmy git. I doubt I could have liked him in any circumstances whatsoever. He was that awful stereotype of the little-big-man, making up for his height by being a complete and utter twat."

"Don't hold back, James. Say what you really mean!" chuckled Melissa.

"No, he was! And he was also the stereotype of a double glazing salesman. That she swapped me out for him added another painful dimension to it all. That she'd not said anything and never given me a chance either? Well that hurt. I think everyone deserves a chance. There was no respect and no feeling in the way that she performed the deed and she had the temerity to say she *hadn't wanted to hurt me.*"

James looked at his hands and saw they were shaking with the emotion of the recollection, "people who avoid difficult situations and conversations make it a hell of a lot worse."

"Bad things happen when good people do nothing?" said Melissa.

James tried for that smile again, it was strained, but it came easier this time, "something like that."

"What happened at the end then?"

"She unceremoniously dumped me and that, as they say, was that."

"What? No further contact at all?"

"Nope. I saw her occasionally, but that was it. You see, she'd already talked it all out."

"Who with?"

"An imaginary version of me in her head..."

"Ouch!"

"Yeah, it's probably more common than I give it credit for, but pretty screwed up all the same."

"A variation on what you'd been doing all along…" quipped Melissa.

"What?" James blurted the word out testily, composing himself and relaxing before continuing, "I hadn't thought about it like that."

"That's why talking about things helps," explained Melissa.

"Yes, I suppose you're right," smiled James.

Melissa grinned, "I make a habit of being right. I have to, to keep you on your toes, matey!"

James' smile broadened, "What I did know, eventually, once I'd put some space between me and that particular car crash, was that I needed that. That what we had wasn't real."

Melissa nodded, "what about the rebounds?"

James eyed her before answering, tried an unsuccessful opening gambit anyway, "who said there was a rebound."

Melissa laughed at his attempt to head her off, "Rebound? No, matey-blokey. I said *rebounds* as in the plural!"

James thought carefully before answering, "there's a lot in life that you don't think about until afterwards isn't there?"

"Your pet theory that retrospect is a curse?"

"It's not...!" James had bitten and he saw a twinkle in Melissa's eyes, "we can all be wise after the event, can't we?" He put on a comedy voice, "oh, you didn't want to do it like that!"

She nodded her agreement and smiled at his joke.

"I thought I was a grown up after that bad experience and I played at being grown up. Thinking that you're all grown up and mature is one of the most childish and foolhardy things you can do. I did a hell of a lot of growing up in my twenties and I was nowhere near ready for a lasting relationship until I made it into my thirties. Only I didn't know it at the time."

"So you broke a few hearts along the way?"

"Yeah..." he sighed, he wasn't proud of that aspect of his life.

"And you were always wary of getting hurt, so you held a part of yourself back and eventually you self-destructed and broke the relationship up."

James sat back, agog at his wife's observation, "what makes you say that?!"

"You're my husband, James! I know you pretty well! I've seen you look at that front door when things aren't going your way.

It's the classic fight or flight instinct, when we've fought, I've seen your barely supressed urge to flight."

It was James' turn to reach out and take his wife's hand, "I may have done quite a bit of growing up in my twenties, but what I realised was that, I would never stop growing up. That was the point. I had to acknowledge that and understand myself better, that I wasn't the finished article and never would be. Maybe I have looked at the door, it's an option for both of us isn't it? Maybe I understood just as well that you could just as easily walk out of that door. That nothing in life is certain or set in stone and that you have to work hard at things come what may."

Melissa squeezed his hand back, "well it is now though isn't it?"

*Set in stone.* Yes, he supposed she was right on that score.

He looked intently at her. She was smiling, but there was a sadness in her eyes. Yes, there was an inevitability to their lives now. She was that inevitability, or rather a version of her was. At least they had time and they knew the score, that was more than most people had, and they were already taking steps together in that time that they had left. He brought his other hand over to join the first, covering her hand completely.

"I love you," he said, and he meant it in a way he had never meant it before. More deeply and fully than he could ever have known.

She saw it in him and she felt it too, "I love you too, you crazy fool."

Then she burst out laughing, her tears falling freely as she grieved. As she began the process of saying goodbye to James and her life.

# 17

Helen was outside the care home as James approached. He watched her perform the ritual of rolling her own, thin cigarette. She had it down to a fine art and she only saw him as she sealed the paper of a perfectly cylindrical roll-up.

"You're good at that," James nodded at the unlit cigarette.

"Plenty of practice," smiled Helen, "want one?"

James considered this for a moment, "yeah, why not?"

"Because you don't smoke?" guessed Helen.

James grinned, "if I was ever going to take smoking up, now is the time isn't it?"

Helen nodded, there was merit in that.

"Besides, I can watch you roll another, it's fascinating to watch."

"Here, hold this then," she passed the already made cigarette to James.

As she undertook the ritual another time she glanced up at him as he watched her intently, "it's more difficult to do this when I know I'm being watched. I'm all fingers and thumbs now!"

"You don't seem to be," chuckled James.

When she'd finished she lit her own cigarette and drew deeply on it, "you're sure about this? I mean, I could keep that one for later?"

James shook his head and put the cigarette in his mouth. It was his turn to feel self-conscious. He felt awkward with the cigarette and thought it probably showed, he certainly wasn't the Man With No Name, cigarillo hanging from his curled lip. She held the lighter to the end of the cigarette the flame licking at the thin paper. He drew on it and watched the flame move toward him slightly.

CHOKE!

James had a coughing fit that took over his body and went at it hard with the convulsions. Eventually, through water filled eyes he noticed Helen watching him carefully.

"Thought that might happen," she said, "now the trick is to get back on the horse if you're serious about this, or to put the thing out and walk away. That's the more sensible option."

James though, could be pig-headed and he placed the rollie back in his mouth. This time around, the smoke wasn't as much of a shock to the system and he managed to swallow down his urge to cough and choke. The rest of the cigarette was less of a challenge.

He could get used to this, he thought, but he knew he'd likely pass up on the opportunity to become a seasoned smoker. Smoking wasn't for him. It just didn't sit right with him.

"So how's it going?" asked Helen.

"Fine," James shrugged.

"Fine?" Helen was pushing back, she wanted more than *fine*. James wasn't here to cough one of his lungs out and tell her things were fine. Things were far from fine. James' life was in a state as far away from fine as could be. That was why he was here. To get away, but not to get away too far. Helen got that. He was here to look at his life in a slightly different way, this was an attempt to understand it, to get it.

"Shall we grab a brew?" she tilted her head towards the door.

James nodded and followed her in.

"So?" she asked as she handed him a mug of steaming tea a few minutes later.

James thought about it for a moment, "Some of it starts being a part of life doesn't it? You just get on with it. You only notice the stand out stuff."

Helen nodded, that was life and that was how it worked.

"That makes it more difficult to describe it and I suppose some things can creep up on you..."

"That's why it's important to think about it and talk about it. You have to keep an eye on things and properly consider them." Helen took a sip of her tea and eyed James from over the top of her mug.

James could see the merit in this. That was probably a part of why he was here. He needed to talk about it and in that talking there was a kind of acceptance and reassurance.

He smiled, "she's started to mix her words up."

"Sometimes that's called a word salad," said Helen, "occasionally people sound like Yoda."

James smiled at that, "I can still understand her meaning. It gave me a jolt the first couple of times, but I sussed it out and usually, she doesn't know she's doing it, so we muddle along fine."

"No big mishaps then?" asked Helen, getting straight to it.

"Mostly no," James drew in a deep breath, this one was clean and he didn't have a choking fit, "I found her sat in the dark the other night."

"Oh. Some people do go for a wander sometimes. You're best bolting doors and making it tricky for any late night wanderings."

James nodded, thankfully they had bolts and deadlocks in place already.

"That wasn't the worst of it though."

Helen waited for him to continue.

"She'd been sitting at her laptop. I don't know how long she'd been there, but when I found her, it had gone into sleep mode. I don't think it had been like that for long."

"You saw what was on the laptop?" asked Helen.

"Yeah, she was looking up how you die from dementia…"

"Oh dear, that's not good…"

"I know, it hurts just thinking about it."

Helen nodded, "Sometimes it's best not to know some things. I mean, the residents here. They know enough. They know they're nearing the end of their lives and I think most of them accept that they've done OK. They've buried friends and family, some of them have buried children. Some people know when it's their time and you see that acceptance. They've made their peace and you can see that they are ready and they… just go. The next generation are going to come here with phones and tablets and create merry havoc! They say you should never Google medical symptoms, that's all that's going to happen isn't it!?"

James smiled despite himself.

"The problem with that," continued Helen, "is that the focus shifts away from the here and now. People forget to live in the moment and enjoy their life, instead they're pushing themselves into that final and horrible ending." She smiled as she recollected something, "I read Julius Caesar at school, you know, Shakespeare?"

James nodded, he'd read it too. Been to a couple of performances as well.

"There's a speech he makes about mortality. Says something about how a man dies a thousand deaths if he worries about his end, whereas a brave man, a man who does not concern himself with the inevitability of death will die but once."

"He was a bit of a pompous git though wasn't he?" said James.

Helen chuckled, "yeah, but he had a point. We might find ourselves worrying about dying, but we have to snap out of it."

"You mean, 'cheer up! It might not happen!'?" James said in a mockney voice.

"Well, we both know it's always going to happen, but not necessarily the way we think it is. Worrying about it will only make it worse."

James drank more of his tea.

"It's not good though is it? And I don't know how to bring it up. I mean it's drawing attention to something that would be best left well alone."

"Probably best leave it be then.  I find people talk about something when they are good and ready, so better to leave it with them so they can find the right time to talk about it if they want to."

"What if she doesn't bring it up?" there was a pitch to James' voice that indicated that he was wound up and worried, that he wasn't happy with where this was.

"Then she doesn't want to talk about it. Would you?" Helen gave him a gently challenging look.

"No... I suppose not..."

Helen nodded, "sometimes the hardest thing to do is to do nothing. Even when you know it's the right thing. Only, it's easy to forget that you are doing something. You're there for her and you're caring and supporting. That's enough."

"Is it though?" asked James.

Helen put her mug down, "I hope so, I've devoted my life to doing just that."

"Sorry... I didn't mean..."

"I know. Believe me, I *do* know. When you care about someone, you want to take it all away. The pain and the suffering. You can't bear to see them like that. Imagine if you could though? You'd be God wouldn't you? And even He doesn't pull that shit. He doesn't intervene in each individual life. That would be cheating and it would rob people of free will, of any semblance of life as we know it."

James frowned, "I didn't know you were religious?"

"I'm not," Helen paused and thought again, "not in the organised and ram it down your throat way anyway. I do believe in God though, and I've seen what that belief can do for people. It's gives much needed perspective and helps people think about something other than themselves. The people here are closer to God than you and I."

"I hadn't thought about it like that before," said James.

"Well, that's what this is all about isn't it?"

James looked puzzled.

"Us talking. Trying to make sense of things and look at things in a better way. If we didn't do this, we would go mad wouldn't we?"

"Or we'd live in blissful ignorance!" grinned James.

"Do you think?" Helen meant this question, it wasn't a rhetorical quip.

"Well some people do..." ventured James.

"You don't though, do you?"

"No, and neither do you."

Helen stood up and collected his mug, "because we both care," she sighed as she said this and then left the room to take the mugs to the kitchen and give them a clean. In the doorway she paused, "you know your way to the lounge don't you?"

She didn't wait for an answer.

# 18

He couldn't help himself.

He had to know.

Melissa was napping downstairs. He went upstairs, finding himself creeping like a thief in the night, and he supposed that that was exactly what he was. He stepped carefully through the detritus that had accumulated once again on the bedroom floor, and he knelt down at the edge of the bed and reached for the box.

His hand scrabbled around for the box, but not finding it, scrabbled further and more urgently. He leant down so his cheek was against the carpet. He couldn't see anything, so he sat back up and pulled his phone from his pocket, flicking the screen upwards and selecting the torch icon. He leant back down and shone the torch under the bed thinking that Melissa must have absently kicked the box further under.

Nothing.

The box was gone.

James sat up and looked around the bedroom as though the shoebox would be there before him in an obvious and conspicuous place and of course this was possible. It was also possible that the box could be almost anywhere, and that included the possibility that it could also be in its original hiding place.

Had Melissa hidden it? Yes, James knew she must have. This was her secret and she would keep it in a place that was only meant for her. But where?

James stood up and sighed. Hands on his hips, he scanned the room again. A search of Melissa's possible hiding places seemed a bridge too far. Even when his evil imp told him he'd find it sooner or later, that when he was going through Melissa's things after she'd gone he would find it then, so why not now? Even then, James put aside his search. If it turned up during his tidying sessions, then sobeit, that was fine, but to search for it and try to discover Melissa's hiding place, that was crossing a line. That was betrayal.

Instead, James turned his attentions to the clothes and objects on the bedroom floor and began tidying them, and as he did so he wondered at the now disappeared box.

How had Melissa known that it was there?

James dismissed that thought. He could send himself crazy following that thread and he was already going crazy with curiosity about Melissa's past life. He had to let this go, he had to content himself in knowing that it was a part of her and that should be good enough for him, because he loved her and that was that. If and when she wanted to talk about it, she would.

As he finished tidying the bedroom, he couldn't help one last glance around the room. He wondered what he would have done should he have spotted the shoe box's hiding place. Knew that he wouldn't have resisted the urge to look inside and read that final letter. He was glad that he had stopped and thought, and ceased his search. That, he knew, was the right thing to do.

He returned downstairs. In the living room he stopped and quietly watched his slumbering wife. He wondered how he could ever truly know another person? Hell, he had forgotten more about himself than he now knew or remembered, and he had a habit of surprising himself. What he did know was that he loved this woman and she was the product of all her past experiences. That was what he'd fallen in love with and that was what he loved now. That she had chosen to spend the rest of her life with him was enough. It was more than enough and he counted himself blessed for her choosing him.

As he gazed upon her, Melissa's face was peaceful, he could image her younger self right now. No cares or worries, happy to exist in the moment, safe and protected by those around her. He was her family now and he'd do his best to keep her safe and to care for her. Right now that was his sole purpose. She stirred, he stayed motionless, fearful of waking her. She settled again, so he crept out of the room. There was plenty to do while she slept.

* * *

"How long was I asleep?" she asked as she padded into the kitchen.

"Not long," smiled James, "about an hour."

He got up from the kitchen table and put the kettle on.

She looked at his laptop and the papers beside it.

"What you up to?" she asked as he made them both a mug of tea.

"Bit of admin to start with and once I'd done with that I thought I'd check in with work."

"Ah," said Melissa guardedly.

She was not privy to James' big conversation with his partner Simon and so she didn't know how badly it had gone, but she wasn't a fan of the overbearing man and had always been wary of him. She kept her antagonism between herself and James, not wanting to contribute to what she saw as an already bad situation, at least as far as James was concerned.

"Thought I'd best dial in and see what was what. Check my emails and head anything major off at the pass," explained James casually.

180

"And was there anything to head off at the pass?"

"No, not really, apart from the usual bollocks," James hoped that Melissa missed the edge in his voice.

There was always going to be something. That was a universal truth when it came to taking time off from work, what could happen would happen. It was like it waited until you were gone before it all unravelled. Usually, once the dust had settled and things were back on an even keel, these things amounted to nothing more than an annoyance. What James had discovered amounted to more than an annoyance and his reliance on the business ticking along with Simon at the helm and James dialling in and keeping a quiet eye on proceedings had been shattered. He didn't know what Simon was playing at, but he intended to find out and put a stop to any nonsense as soon as he could.

He handed Melissa her tea.

"Shall we?" he asked her as he took his seat, closed his laptop and lifted his papers to one side to reveal a writing pad.

She smiled at her husband and shook her head in mock disbelief, "if we have to..." she said in lacklustre protest.

"We do," he said sternly, "now if you're sitting comfortably, we will begin!"

Melissa cleared her throat, "In the beginning, I was small, but I was fierce. Mother and Father had wanted a little girl, but instead they got me. I may have looked like a little girl. They may have dressed me like a little girl and treated me as such, but when I was in motion, it was very clear that I was anything but a little girl..."

"So what were you then?" James' eyes were twinkling, he liked the start of this story.

"Shhh! I'm mid-flow!" She waved a hand at him to encourage him to desist.

He did just that, she had retained some of her fierceness and ferocity. Mostly James was in the eye of her storm and he only ever saw flashes of it, and that was enough. That said, the same fire, grit and determination was deployed when Melissa had the bit between her teeth and wanted things done. She could be a force of nature at times and James knew that this could be both good and bad. Most of it was good and that scoring worked for James. Things came out in the wash and that meant their life together was mostly good. James didn't think you could or should expect anything more than that. If you raised the bar too high then you were dooming things to hurt and failure.

"My Uncle Bill used to say, in a stage whisper, that the hospital was next door to a vets and there had been a terrible mix up, that somewhere there was a sweet little girl who was being sent down rabbit holes to flush out the fluffy creatures for the gamekeepers tea. In keeping with my true nature as a working terrier, I would chase my Uncle and more than once I managed to leave teeth marks on his arm or leg. That I was still doing this into my teens was a source of concern and consternation to both my parents. I don't know which was the more disappointed, my Mother for my letting her gender down and for my not being a chip off her block, or my Father for my not really being a daddy's girl. You see I was independent from an early age and that independence was mistaken for waywardness…"

James laid his pen down, "you're being serious aren't you?" he asked.

"Deadly," she gave nothing away with her expression, "did no one warn you? Not even when you asked my Father for my hand in marriage?"

James shook his head cautiously.

Melissa shrugged, "I suppose they must've assumed you knew by then!"

"So you were quite a handful as a child?"

"You could say that," agreed Melissa, "it didn't help that I struggled with some aspects of education."

James knew that she was mildly dyslexic, but that this hadn't been identified or acknowledged until well into her teens. With Melissa's story unfolding, he guessed that her underperformance at school in certain of the subjects was mistaken for her over exuberance and lack of focus.

"You didn't struggle with some aspects of education though, did you?"

"No, I had an *eye* for things and I loved to draw and to create. If I was interested in something, then I'd soak that subject up like a sponge. The problem was that my interests were rarely academic," she giggled.

"OK, that's good background, but you must have stories?" prompted James.

"Alright, buster! Hold your horses!" she stroked her chin theatrically.

"When I was eight, I fell off a horse."

"I didn't know you rode?" said James.

"I didn't."

James frowned.

"I was supposed to be playing in the back garden, but I got bored of playing there, so I played in the front garden instead and then I got bored of that, so I went for a walk and on my walk I spotted a horse and it was next to the fence, so I climbed the fence and then I climbed onto the horse. The horse wasn't expecting this and I certainly wasn't expecting it to leg it before I was properly seated. So as I lay across its back it ran across the field. Then it stopped and I didn't."

"Oh," said James.

"Oh indeed," agreed Melissa, "I must've looked a sight as I span through the air. I know I looked a sight after that because my Mother's face was a picture. I had blood down the side of my face as I walked into the kitchen saying, 'Mummy! I fell!'."

Melissa parted her hair to reveal a scar, "Have I really not told you this before?"

"No! And I haven't seen that before!" protested James.

"Five stitches that," she smiled proudly, "how I didn't split my head open more often, I really don't know. I certainly had plenty of opportunity to. I was an avid climber you see. Mostly trees, but I also managed to get on the roof of Uncle Bill's house once too."

"I take it he didn't live in a bungalow?" tried James.

"No, Uncle Bill wasn't a bungalow kind of dude, his pad was a nineteen thirties semi with nice big, cast iron downpipes, made for climbing!"

"Why don't I know any of this?!" wailed James.

Melissa shrugged, "I suppose it never came up. I didn't know about you crashing your green Lotus and having macabre dreams about leg wounds until the other day," she smiled at her husband, "am I putting you off me?"

"Never," grinned James.

"Oh!" cried Melissa rubbing her hands together and warming to her theme, "you shouldn't have said that!"

Then she proceeded to tell James the story of a summer in the countryside and her mistaking a cesspit on a nearby farm for a pool. So she went for a dip. James began to wonder how Melissa had made it into adulthood alive, let alone in one piece.

What he didn't know at that point was that Melissa had only just begun with her stories of derring-do, high jinks and adventure...

# 19

J ames knew as soon as he walked into the office.

Something felt off. It felt wrong. Very wrong. He tried to rationalise and dismiss this feeling, he was bound to feel odd having stepped away and in such circumstances. It was too much to expect that he would swan back into the office and for it to feel like he'd never been away. He might even have romanticised his visit and his eventual return, seeing himself as Tom Hanks in the opening credits of a film he once saw. Bright vibrant music accompanying his cheery entry into the building, waving, smiling and greeting his fellow office workers by name and making little quips here and asking the most pertinent of questions there, because Tom knew everyone and more importantly? He cared, and because he cared everyone couldn't help but love him.

Well James cared too, but in a more reserved, more substantial and so, far deeper way. This was his business and he'd built it from nothing. This was not only his livelihood, but also the main source of income for all the people who worked here. He felt a profound obligation to all of them not to stuff it up so they could all rely on this business and focus instead on their lives. No one needed that uncertainty in their lives and they certainly didn't deserve having the rug pulled from under them. James had been there and that was why he went through all the pain and stress of striking out on his own, but at least he had his good friend Simon with him near the start. Not at the outset, James had already done a lot of the groundwork and the business was underway when Simon joined him, they figured that twice the input would take them further and more quickly and so Simon joined in order to grow the business. In the early days, James had joked about Simon being Employee Number One. Simon had not taken kindly to that joke and had always firmly corrected it, he was not an employee, he was a director and he was James' business partner.

Simon was walking out of his office, putting his jacket on as James crossed the office floor.

"James..." he cleared his throat and struggled to get his arm through the sleeve of his jacket, it were as though some wag had stitched the sleeve closed when he wasn't looking, "I thought we were meeting around the corner, at that pub you suggested?"

James smiled despite the wave of nausea he felt. That bad feeling he'd picked up on as he walked into the office had intensified as he saw Simon's reaction to seeing James here in the office. Sometimes you just knew, and right now, James knew. He could see it writ large upon Simon's face. He could see it in his eyes. Eyes that were darting all over the place as they avoided James.

Simon looked shifty.

Simon *never* looked shifty. Simon was the bullish, ultra-confident one. He didn't have charisma as much as bluster and swagger. Simon was, as they say, a force of nature. Not this Simon though. This Simon was shifty, uncomfortable and James thought, *guilty as hell.*

He brushed past James, still waggling his arm around in an attempt to get it through the intransigent sleeve. At that rate, he was going to tear the arm off the jacket or do himself an injury. James had no inclination to say anything nor to help him. Instead he stood his ground.

"Come on, let's go to the pub!" Simon tried for cheery, but missed the mark so that it sounded like a barked order.

James watched him finally succeed in getting his arm all the way into his jacket. Simon had stopped to focus on this simple act of dressing himself. He'd also stopped as he'd spotted that James was not following him.

James stared at his friend, the intensity of his gaze boring into him.

"What?" said Simon, continuing to avoid his gaze.

"As I'm here, let's have a wee chat in my office, eh Simon?" James watched his friend carefully as he made the suggestion that was far from a mere suggestion.

"No. Let's go to the pub, I dunno about you, but I'm thirsty!"

"All in good time, Simon. We'll go to the pub, I just want five minutes here first."

Simon's jaw set. James observed the change in the man. Simon was a fighting man. Nonetheless he'd tried flight, but James hadn't cooperated, so now he was going to fight. James didn't give him a chance to launch into whatever he was about to do, he turned on his heel and went in the direction Simon had come from.

Simon trailed in his wake. Flapping. James didn't turn back to see this, he could hear it and strangely, he sensed it. It were as though his senses were suddenly enhanced. He had a clarity not often afforded him and he doubted few ever had this total sense of *knowing*. He thought it would send a person mad to be this aware for any length of time. He could feel his body humming, nearly fizzing with energy and the periphery of his too clear vision seemed to blur and shake as though he or the world around him was thrumming with electricity. Sound also was strange to him. He felt more alive than he had ever been and yet alien. Worse still, he felt a tremendous far off sadness that presently sat outside of this experience, but he knew that what he was experiencing was transitory and it would soon enough be replaced with that waiting sadness. A sadness that he would have to deal with on top of everything else he had to deal with in his life.

A part of him was regretting today and him ever coming to the office. That part, he knew, was a weak part of him. A part that

190

didn't want to show up most days because life could be hard and it didn't want things ever to be hard. The rest of him had to contend with that dissent and muster even more motivation to face the day, come what may.

James' temporary sense of knowing extended to the ajar office door he was approaching. He knew that this door led onto a space that was no longer his own and in knowing this, he knew that it was not only the office that was no longer his. Nonetheless, he strode into that office with a sense of purpose that was no longer his own, driven forth by this strange force that had taken him over and filled him with vital energy and purpose.

"...listen, can I call you back," said a man behind the desk that had once been James' desk.

He placed his phone down on his desk very deliberately and glowered at James, "and who are you?!"

James, in his currently detached-from-the-world state, found this interesting. Ordinarily, when someone walked into an office unannounced, the occupant of the office would be curios and say something like *can I help you.* This man, this man who looked like a private equity fund man, the kind of guy that, were you to snap him in half would have *corporate* write through him like an awful stick of seaside rock candy, went straight for aggressive. Behind him was Simon, flapping around like a guilty teenager; *no! Don't go in there Mum!* Don't go in there, because you'll discover something really embarrassing.

This must be what it feels like to come home one evening and discover your wife in flagrante. Driven forth on legs that were not your own to discover what you already knew in your heart of hearts...

*Betrayal.*

This, thought James, is *the other man.* And the reason that he is aggressive, or at the very least defensive, is that he knew that this day was coming. He knows very well who I am!

James, still under the spell of *knowing*, did something he'd never usually do. He parked his bum on his former desk and took upon himself a seemingly casual pose. As casual as it may have seemed, it was about as possessive and provocative as it came. James wasn't only owning the desk, he was owning the moment and everything in it.

With a calm he did not feel within, but that came through in any case, he spoke.

"You know perfectly well who I am," he extended his hand, "I'm James, yes *the* James. And you are?"

The man behind the desk automatically shook James' hand. James could see that he was regretting this as soon as it was happening, but it was such a deeply embedded habit that he couldn't help himself, instead he went for defiance in a different guise.

"None of your business," he crowed.

James was not predisposed to like the man, after all, he was in cahoots with Simon, and this reaction and in particular the crowing was uncalled for, but in keeping with this type of corporate rat. Uncalled for and callous were trademarks of a person like this.

"Well, Mr None of Your Business, I am so pleased to put a face to the name!"

James let go of the man's hand and took to his feet, he smiled a smile at Simon who was stood in the doorway and then turned the same smile on the man with the unusual name.

"Only..." he put a finger to his chin to telegraph a moment of deep thought.

"I expected you to say that your name is Timothy Argyle... I take it you're the kind of guy who doesn't go in for truncating your name. You're a full blown *Timothy* aren't you?" James managed to make the man's name sound like something soiled and despicable, the effect was rewarding. Timothy did not want to reply and instead his mouth made movements like a fish out of water, for as of now, that was exactly what he was.

James was having his moment. Not often does a person get to have their moment. Moments usually pass and in passing they only then make themselves known as the allotted slot for a person to have done something about the ignominy of life that has occurred. To spot the moment and to fill it well was rare indeed.

"And where is Brian? Is he in the office today?"

James looked askance at Timothy who just glowered at him, then he turned his questioning look towards Simon. Simon saw the movement and averted his eyes before James' own were upon him.

James stood there and let things hang. Eventually he returned his gaze to Timothy, "well, nice to meet you, *Timmy*."

He couldn't help himself, didn't know he was going to do it until it was said, Timmy came out in an approximation of the South Park character's voice. Timothy winced as though struck with the word. His glowering intensified. James willed him to react further. Just you bloody try it, buster, he thought to himself and something of that thought must have telegraphed itself to Timothy as he averted his gaze and ceased his glowering.

James turned to his former friend and nodded his head past the door. Simon looked relieved, taking this as a signal that James had had enough and wanted to leave the offices.

Simon was wrong.

"Thank you," James said as he maintained his casual air and exited his former office. The office with a cuckoo called Timothy sitting in it.

James headed towards the exit door with Simon trailing behind him. He aimed deliberately at the door and at the last moment he performed a perfectly timed and executed shimmy. He'd never been any good at rugby, but that side step was worthy of a rugby international and it certainly wrong footed the already beleaguered Simon.

To one side of the exit door was the door to the main, open plan office. The door that James was even now opening and passing through. If anyone had thought that James had had his moment in Timothy's office they were sorely mistaken, for that was only the warm up act. This was James' moment, for these were James' people. He had taken on each and every one of them and made them part of this team. He had spoken to them and told them of his vision and his expectations for the journey that they would undertake together. He had been very particular about the nature of the relationship that they would have from day one, that he was intent on avoiding the trap of *becoming an employer,* that he had to remember why it was that he had set this firm up and why they were all here. It was about doing a good job and getting things done, but it was equally about trust and allowing people to flourish. There was no clock card system. There was no expectation that people absolutely must be in the office at a given time and stay until another, pre-allotted time, there was not even an expectation that they had to be in the office... the freedoms and the respect and the arrangements that applied to James applied to all. They would do this the right way so they could build not only a great and thriving business that provided them with fulfilment and security, but also great lives that entwined around their work and were not impacted and even broken as a result of the inflexible demands of a workplace policed with people who didn't care and didn't bother to even try to get it.

That was a big part of James's vision and as he walked into the work area shared by all the team, including himself, his office being a sometime break out area for meetings and quiet moments, he saw as well as felt the extent of Simon's betrayal. That he had indulged James and paid lip service to his vision, such that at the earliest possible opportunity, he made draconian changes that rendered this place yet another backward and horrible workplace. A space and time to be tolerated, not enjoyed.

All the desks were filled. No one was working remotely. The only thing to be said for that was that it meant that James had a full house for his performance. He felt the awaiting sadness more clearly now, it had ramped up a level as he felt the atmosphere in this room and it loomed large, threatening to overwhelm him.

He stood there, unnoticed at first, and then people began to look up and his heart broke as he saw the hope in their eyes and felt the buzz of excitement at the sight of him. James had returned! All was not lost after all!

James hadn't known what he was going to say, only that he was going to say something, now though as he became the focus of these expectant eyes he couldn't bring himself to give forth of a torrent of vitriol. Although that had never been James' style and what he had expected that he would do was merely tell it like it was. The naked truth of it was ugly enough for all to see.

Now though, he could see that very truth in the eyes of his team. They already knew and him saying it out loud would do them no favours, in fact all it would do was needlessly hurt them. That was too much for James, none of them deserved that.

"Hi everyone!" he beamed a smile as he said these words. His face lighting up. This was genuine and heartfelt, he was so glad to see them all, "how the hell are you all doing?"

There was a general murmur across the office that conveyed a lacklustre and half-hearted *we're alright, thanks.* The British were really good at this. It was all part and parcel of the stiff upper lip and putting a brave face on things. Ask a Brit how they are doing, even in the midst of them being cut to pieces by pirates and eaten alive from below by a swarm of rabid sharks and they'll give you a cheery response, *mustn't grumble!*

"Lovely to see you all again, I'm on a flying visit, but I'll have to come back and maybe we can go out for lunch and a catch up?" he also said this with that beaming smile, but he knew this wasn't going to happen. That he would never set foot in this office ever again.

That he would see them all again though? He had no doubt of that. He intended to see each and every one of them again and in happier circumstances. He could see that now, and that impending sadness receded a touch as a result. It was still there and he knew it lay in wait and would hit him hard, but it had already lost some of its power and in so doing, James now knew that he would win this particular battle and come out the other side. That this sadness was a passing fancy and something that he could endure because he had the beginnings of a plan and he'd had a plan such as this once before, a plan that had resulted in the creation of this business.

He turned back towards the door and nodded at Simon. The nod was very deliberate and the movement itself seemed to throw meaning across the room from James to Simon. It was something that was witnessed by everyone present and was the twin of the truth that everyone already knew. With it, James marked Simon. Marked him in front of all the people that now worked for him.

"Shall we go?" he said to Simon.

It wasn't a question.

It was an order.

And Simon duly followed James meekly from the office.

# 20

"You did what!?" Helen was incredulous at what she had just heard.

COUGH!

This time it was her coughing, not James. She doubled over and the coughing turned to retching, James reached over automatically and patted her back firmly.

"Are you alright?" he asked as she straightened up again.

Her face was flushed with the coughing fit and she had a peculiar expression.

"Yeah..." she chuckled and coughed once more, "you're a revelation! You know that? I mean... you just caught me off guard and I was laughing, but should I be laughing? Is this... I'm sorry! The mental image you conjured. I'm so glad you did that James! And thank you for telling me. You've made my day!"

James had told her about his visit to the office. She had asked for his news and he'd told her matter-of-factly about it. No embellishment, he'd just recounted his visit.

"And you went to the pub with him?" she now asked.

"Yeah, that was the original arrangement, and I figured Simon had a script prepared. That was where I was going to hear his ever so slightly biased account of what had happened..."

"How was that?" she asked.

She was rolling another rollie.

"A second?" asked James.

"Yeah," she pointed to the ground where her first was laying, half smoked.

"Oh..." James frowned, "sorry about that."

"It's fine," she grinned at him, "just warn me next time you're going to drop something like that, OK?"

James returned the grin.

"Go on then! What was your so-called friend's story? Why did he think it was OK... to do what he did."

And James told her.

20

They had gone to the Red Lion. Where else? James had to go back, the place intrigued him. He was realistic enough to think that his first visit was a complete one off and that any attempt at replication would be futile. However, that first visit was evidence of two characters who James would like to see again. Besides, he liked the pub and in a strange way, it felt like his territory.

He took a seat outside. He drew a line at introducing Simon to the insides of the Red Lion. Outside was as close as Simon was getting. Other than heading to the bar to sort their drinks.

"Guinness please, Simon." James nodded to the door of the pub.

Simon had been in the process of taking a seat opposite James. He was in that awkward half down, but still half up, leaning at an angle pose. He stopped like that. James thought it was probably very good for his core strength. Then Simon rose again.

"Right... yes... OK..."

As he turned to walk into the pub, James spoke again.

"Oh, and I'll have a double Jameson's chaser."

Simon turned back towards James, thought about saying

something about the unusual request of a stiff chaser, that it wasn't like the James that he knew, but thought better of it as he saw the steely look on James face. The whole situation was unusual and it would not do to draw attention to it. Things were not panning out at all the way Simon had expected.

James wondered at the man. How did he expect things to turn out?!

Simon returned with the drinks, he'd bought a lager for himself, "odd place this," he observed, "never even knew it existed."

"Yes," replied James. He was glad Simon hadn't warmed to the Red Lion, he hadn't thought that it was Simon's cup of tea, but it was reassuring to know that it was unlikely he would ever be back.

James response didn't give Simon much to go on and they lapsed into a moment's silence, drinking from their pints for something to do. Having had a good gulp of his Guinness, James lifted the tumbler of whiskey and swilled it around, sniffing it and savouring the aroma. The smell of the whiskey hinted at the warmth the drink would bestow as it entered the mouth and slipped downwards. James then poured the lot into his Guinness, noting Simon's horrified look and not giving a shit about it. Mostly he was in a not giving a shit mood and Simon was exceedingly lucky that he was. James had a momentary thought about how else this could be playing out and the theme for that alternative was *unpleasant.* Even now, the theme was *unpleasant,* only the unpleasantness resided entirely within Simon, James hadn't given him the wriggle room to provoke him and to draw something out into the open that they could both focus on instead of what Simon had done.

James took a drink from his whiskey enhanced pint and savoured the taste and the feeling of that warmth. Usually, there would be the promise of a reassuring kind of numbness, a glow, an insulation from the harsh realities of life. James knew that the whiskey could not go that far today. He doubted he'd feel that glow, nor experience true merriment in his cups for some time to come.

"So," he said, moving the proceedings along to the business they had between them.

So...

What the hell could Simon say to justify this? James waited and watched his friend. Was he experiencing this control and inner sense of calm because of everything else that was happening in his life? Had Simon's stunt paled into insignificance because Melissa was falling apart? As James thought about this, he felt an overwhelming urge to get up and go to her. This was a waste of his time and none of it mattered. Only, he thought back to a time not all that long ago, a time when this did matter and he thought about his hard work, blood, sweat and tears. The sleepless nights and anguish – was he doing the right thing? And he thought about all those people in that office. His team. That was what counted. Them. In the final analysis, it was always about people. People like Simon would possibly never get that. The Timothys of this world certainly wouldn't, they had sold their humanity early doors and sacrificed the possibility of being a worthwhile part of the human race. They were one dimensional, money grubbing whores, using people up along their ascent up the slippery corporate pole. That Simon had climbed into bed with Timothy was very telling. Very telling indeed.

And sad.

Melissa had been right about Simon all along.

Deep down, James had always known this, but he'd mitigated it with the oft used incantation *but he's my friend.* At best, this was a display of unquestioning and undying loyalty, a noble thing. At worst, it was a cop out and an unwillingness to see things as they really were. Why? Because admitting it was painful. Then there would be the additional pain of having to do something about it.

Well, no need now! Simon had already done something about it...

"You went AWOL..." Simon's delivery of this opener had none of his usual bluster and confidence. James didn't think this was part of the presentation he had prepared and rehearsed. This was mildly encouraging, but he didn't think it would mark a change of heart and reversal of everything Simon had done, things had gone too far along the path for that and Timothy and Brian had their claws in the business now. They would never let go and James could see a future that Simon could not. The karmic wheel was already turning. Simon had made

20

choices that would ensure that he did not come out of this at all well. What would really undo him would be that he wouldn't see it coming. He no longer had a wing man. There was no one around him that he could trust...

"My wife is dying," James said it like it was a fact and it sounded alien to him. It didn't sound *right* even now.

"You say that, but..."

"But what?!" James kept his voice low, but there was steel in those words. They were a warning.

The warning went unheeded. Simon wasn't good at taking heed, had never seen the importance of it.

"Well, it's not like stage four cancer is it!?" the bluster was there now. This was Simon and without someone to handle him and head him off when he was about to do maximum damage, he was a total liability.

James was amazed that he managed to hold it together, he felt detached from the man sat at the bench opposite Simon. He marvelled at the calmness of that man.

"What do you mean?" he invited Simon to expand upon the point he was trying to make.

"Bloody Altzimmers? My gran went on for twenty years with that! She'd always been a bit of a fruitcake. It's no big deal!" Simon was getting a head of steam up now, James let him carry on and watched him as he got himself fired up, "I understand that it's a bit upsetting when someone forgets things, but to give up, grab your coat and take the ball home with you? That's over-egging the pudding isn't it? It's like you went mental too! Twenty years! No business can survive being left in the lurch for twenty weeks, let alone twenty years! AND..."

"And?" James asked.

Simon took a slurp of his lager, his mouth having dried as he delivered his tirade, "And. I'll tell you *and...* she's in her thirties, not some old, dried up biddy who's already had a good innings. Dying!? She'll outlast us all!"

Simon laughed. James watched him steadily as he let forth with this laugh, there was some degree of relief in it. He'd said his piece and he'd justified his position. A position from which he had stolen James' business from under him, silently. Like a thief in the night.

There was the betrayal, that was the ice cold knife that James had felt between his ribs as he discovered Simon's treachery. The thought that followed this was that this wasn't like Simon. Of course, that was a natural thought. No one keeps a person close to them, considers them to be a good friend and go into business with them if they suspect that there will be an act of betrayal on the cards...

It was this though! It was Simon in full flow, spouting whatever he felt like spouting. He was the proverbial bull in a china shop, and yet he'd gone quiet and pulled the plug on James without

206

so much as a by-your-leave. This was not Simon's style.

James laid his hands out on the table. Applied pressure against the table with the palms of his hands. Composing and centring himself.

"I know that you've transferred everything away from me and effectively locked me out of the business..." he began, attempting to use neutral language and keep things as measured as was possible in the circumstances.

He took a deep breath. Was Simon going to furnish him with any explanation? Was he going to tell him the *how* of it or the *why* of it? Did Simon even know anything over and above the fact that James was no longer the owner of his own business?

"And now I know your reasoning..." James added.

He paused.

"Why didn't you talk to me?" he asked his former friend.

That was the obvious question. That was what James wanted to know.

Really, he already knew the answer to how, and that Simon was highly unlikely to tell him because the headline to that one was that it was very illegal indeed. That Simon and his new chums had pulled a fast one.

He also knew the headline to why. That one was easy and it

was obvious. *I did it, because I could.* Sometimes, people did things purely because they could, and sometimes that was a good thing. People climbed mountains because they were there. Unfortunately, people also took things that were not theirs because they could. Simon would learn that lesson the hard way, at the hands of Timothy and Brian. That was how they earned their living. It wasn't about running a business for them, it was about acquiring it by fair means or foul and then turning a quick buck on it. Usually, they got a stake and that was all they needed. Once they were in, they stayed until they had control and then they sold, moved onto the next mark and did it all over again.

Simon shrugged, "what was there to talk about?"

"Really?" James barely managed to keep the emotion out of this challenge.

"You went AWOL..." Simon said this slowly, as though James was hard of thinking, "you abandoned the business... you left me in the lurch... you were no longer of sound mind and I had to do all I could to save the business! My complete focus was on that, not having tea and biscuits with my loopy friend!"

"Loopy?"

"Well... you've obviously lost it... going off the reservation at the first sign of trouble."

"And you came to this conclusion about my sanity, how?"

"I told you! Altzimmers isn't a big deal! Loads of people have it and live to a ripe old age. All this *oh my wife is dying* is total bullshit! I needed you and you weren't there, so I did what I had to!"

"Right... OK... I probably need to put you straight on a couple of things. But before I begin, know this..." he paused to ensure he had Simon's undivided attention, "I was the checks and brakes on you. Without someone to work alongside you and with you... well, you pull things like this. If you're questioning anyone's sanity, you'd be best off looking in the mirror first. The road ahead of you is going to get very bumpy and I pity you. I really do."

"Is that a threat?" growled Simon.

"No, there's no need for threats. Not one bit," James smiled, "now on a couple of points of fact that you would have done well to establish before you embarked upon all of this. Facts you could have gleaned having spoken with me... it's Alzheimer's. That's how you say it. Alzheimer's."

"Whatever," Simon scowled at him. He'd never appreciated being put straight or corrected.

James smiled again. He wasn't enjoying this, but he did enjoy the effect his smile had on Simon, "For the record, Melissa does *not* have Alzheimer's or Altzimmers for that matter. She has early on-set dementia, only she has something that the doctors have never seen before and it's aggressive. It's so aggressive that it will kill her in the next twelve months and for a significant proportion of that time she will not be very well at all. She will be in all sorts of trouble and she will need me. She needs me right now, and I can ill afford this bloody charade with you."

He was shaking now. Mention of Melissa had brought him back to her and to what really counted. This was all noise now and he was better off without it. He was shaking with anger and the injustice of it all; the cruel disease that had entered his life and was taking the one thing he loved above all else away from him.

"Oh..." said Simon, "I didn't know..."

Simon had gone very pale and was leaning back. Keeping his distance. Wary of a visibly angry James. He was frightened. James saw him for what he really was in that moment. A bully and a coward.

"Of course you didn't know," James growled these words, "that's the problem, you didn't know and worse still, you didn't want to know. You didn't bother to find out! What kind of a person does that to a friend?"

Simon didn't respond, other than to avert his eyes and remain leant back, out of harm's way. Not that James was going to attack him. Simon was judging James by his own standards, thinking about how he would react in this situation and what he would do.

"You were the cool kid, Simon. I actually looked up to you. You

20

had the swagger. The confidence to do anything you wanted. It wasn't just that power though. Because it was powerful at times. It was... I remember your bedroom. How we used to sit in your room and make plans for the rest of our lives. In the background, there would be music playing that I had never heard before. I'd ask you what a particular track was and afterwards, I'd look it up and buy the album. You informed a lot of my musical taste. If it was cool, you had it. The clothes, the games. Hell! You even had that poster of the tennis woman scratching her butt, only yours was the Viz woman, not the all too common Athena one. And you had Tank Girl posters. You *read* Tank Girl and 2000AD and you leant me graphic novels like Watchmen and Frank Miller's Bat Man. That was *the* Bat Man. You introduced me to worlds I didn't know existed and you made me feel like anything was possible."

James took a deep breath and his body shuddered with barely contained emotion, a tidal wave of grief at losing his best friend and in such terrible circumstances.

"I was in awe of you, mate. I constantly felt lucky that you had chosen *me!* That the coolest kid on the block wanted to hang out with me, but better still wanted to buddy up with me and take on the world. With you at my side, we could take on the world and actually win! Do things on our terms and bloody well *own it!*"

James looked earnestly at his friend. Now open and questioning. Simon stared back at him and James could see only anger.

"That wasn't me!" Simon hissed, "*you* were the cool kid! What you've just said? That was stuff! That's all it was! Yeah, so I had parents that gave me money so I could go out and buy whatever I wanted. That was the extent to their input in my life. I was lonely and I was bored. Then you came along and you were actually interested in me. Not in my money and what I could buy you. And you have this easy way with you. You can talk to people. I mean *properly* talk to them like they matter and you're interested. I envied you that. Always have..."

James felt deflated by this revelation. Wondered at how he'd never really seen things for how they were. But then, he thought, he had. Simon needed him as much as he had needed Simon. They had complimented each other. That was what friendship was largely about, a bargain that was mutually convenient, only Simon had now destroyed their bargain.

"So what happened, Simon?"

James didn't mean the most recent history. He wasn't after Simon relating the mechanics of how he'd shafted James. James already had a good idea of how that one had played out and knew that Simon would never tell him anyway. He'd probably never revisit that part of his life, in that spot was an emotional veneer and on that veneer was writ large *I was right.* That's what people did to justify something bad. They convinced themselves that they had been right, at least at the time, and that was that. They would never go back. No one would ever understand. That they themselves didn't understand was beside the point.

Simon shrugged, and in that moment he was the teenager that

James had befriended, "You moved on," he said simply.

"I moved on how?" asked James, baffled at this answer of Simon's.

Simon scowled at him, his scowl said *really?*

"Melissa," was all Simon said.

"Melissa?" repeated James.

"Yeah, once she came along, nothing was ever the same again. *And* she never liked me."

James bit his tongue and pushed back on his automatic response to this. Simon was jealous!? This was what it was all about? Simon had had his nose put out of joint and he'd awaited an opportunity to even the score. How base and petty could people be? How easily they could retreat from situations and instead of talking and making the best of what was there before them in the world, they would opt to sulk and talk to themselves and create a bad situation out of an innocuous one. Simon had secretly simmered and built up a head of steam that had ultimately come out in a way which saw James lose his business and his best friend in one fell swoop, but Simon was too blind to see that he was the architect of all of this mess and that he was the biggest loser, for he had not only lost his best friend, he'd swapped that friend for two callous sharks and it was only a matter of time before they would turn on him and take away from him the only thing that he now had left.

For Simon, it was all about the tangible. It was about the business and the money. When he lost that, he would be crushed and James doubted that he would bounce back. He felt sorry for his friend, but didn't see a way back right now. He knew, even in light of what Simon had done, James would always leave the door open to him, but that Simon's pride and anger would ensure that he never walked through that door. If anything, James acceptance of what Simon had done and of Simon would make it even worse for him. Simon would not be able to deal with that, he'd see it as James being the better person and Simon could never lose face.

*People...* thought James, they can be so perverse at times. Their own worst enemies and mostly this was true because they were blind to that fact. You could not help someone who would not be helped and James doubted that Simon would ever darken his door again. It was such a shame.

This was goodbye however James cut it.

"Simon..." James sighed.

"Don't try and paper over the cracks James! Don't tell me I'm wrong!" Simon glowered at him.

There it was, don't tell him he's wrong. Simon was entrenched and nothing James could say or do would make a difference.

He'd say his piece anyway.

"You're my best friend, Simon. Nothing will ever change that.

At the end of it all, the only thing we have is our memories..." these words brought him to a place he didn't want to be right now and he fought the emotion of it, memories was all anyone ever had and to be robbed of them was sacrilege... "I have a wealth of fantastic memories thanks to the times we shared. You brought out the best in me. Look at what we achieved! You'll always have a place in my life and I'm sorry if you felt different. I'm sorry that you never said anything. I thought we were fine. And if there was ever a problem between us I would know. Do you know why I thought that?"

Simon shook his head.

"Because we always saw eye-to-eye. We *talked!*"

"You stopped talking to me when Melissa came along," said Simon churlishly.

"I didn't, but I also didn't see the change in you. We were both busy and I thought we were having fun? The business was going places and so were we. Melissa came along at that stage in my life and everything just sort of fell into place."

"For you maybe. Not for me."

Now Simon was petulant. James felt this inexplicable urge to laugh at his friend looking so childish. Somehow he managed to resist that urge.

"But you never said anything," James stated simply.

Simon glowered, "this isn't on me, James. Don't you even try to do that to me!"

James wasn't going to get dragged into a bun fight. It would be so easy to state the bleeding obvious. It was on Simon. All he had to do was say something, and Simon was the one who had stolen the business that James had started from scratch, but were James to point out these simple facts of life, Simon would only get more angry and entrench himself further. Afterwards, all Simon would remember was his anger and that James had provoked that anger in him.

James raised his hands in a placatory manner, "Fair enough."

He got to his feet, "all I want you to know Simon is…"

He paused. Simon had become even more defensive. Simon was expecting James to take a final, decisive parting shot. Perhaps make a threat. Declare war.

He didn't.

James shrugged earnestly as he stood at the bench looking down at his friend, "you're my mate. I love you to bits. I'll always be there. You know where I am."

Simon looked up at James. He looked confused. Then the fight left him and he looked somehow diminished. For a brief moment, he looked like he was about to say something. A flame of hope flickered in James' chest. If ever there was a moment to pull this back from the brink, it was here and now, Simon just had to give forth of those words that were even now on his lips. Then he thought better of it and drew back, crossing his arms as he did.

Simon said nothing and instead nodded curtly.

\* \* \*

"And that as they say, was that" said James to Helen.

"Wow!" said Helen.

They were in the office. Both of their mugs of tea had gone cold as James recounted his story of betrayal, intrigue and woe.

"Wow?" said James.

"You really held it together and didn't give him both barrels?"

"What would be the point?" asked James.

"What wouldn't be the point!?" chuckled Helen.

"Wouldn't have achieved anything, would have just made things worse."

"Worse how?" asked Helen.

James could see her point. As far as Simon and James were

concerned, there was nothing left. Not really. Except...

"Simon and me were friends from our teens. We did everything together. Including creating that business. We saved each other a number of times, pulled each other from the brink, lifted each other when times were bad." James shrugged, "if I'd have given him both barrels. If I'd gone nuclear, then I'd have known exactly what I was doing and there would never have been a way back for either of us. I couldn't write off what we achieved together. I couldn't reduce its value in my life. Besides..."

"Besides?" said Helen.

Was there really more?

"I believe in redemption. I have to believe in that because that's hope right there. The hope that people can be better. If I extinguish that flame then something dies inside me. I become colder. Cynical. And after all that's happening, I can't afford to do that. I suppose I did what I did for me. I needed it to go that way."

"Wow! I'm in the presence of a modern day saint!" chuckled Helen.

"You what?" said James defensively.

"Well, it's all very well you saying all of this, but I don't quite believe it."

"Really?" James was becoming more and more defensive.

Helen either didn't notice or didn't care.

"If you don't mind me saying, it all sound a bit condescending and... what's the word?" asked Helen, mentally reaching for the word that went hand in glove with condescending and not quite getting to it.

"Sanctimonious?" ventured an incredulous James.

"Yes!" Helen clapped her hands, "that's the one!"

She barely noticed James get up, let alone the fact he was seething. She'd managed to press his buttons and rub him up the wrong way and she had missed it because he'd given forth of all those fine words just now and she'd assumed that she was on safe ground. Things don't always play that way and if anything, James was coming down from all of his fine work and was fragile and vulnerable right now. Neither of them had seen this coming which made it all the worse when it did.

"Right, I'd best be off," he said brusquely.

"Oh... OK..." said Helen, caught out at this unexpected announcement and at the speed that James was leaving.

And then he was gone.

Helen watched the door swing shut and only then did she question whether she might perhaps of said the wrong thing.

# 21

"So how did it go?" asked Melissa.

James was taken aback. Melissa's question had come out of the blue. He didn't answer as he wasn't sure as to what Melissa was referring, but that said, as he reached for a possible answer, he had a good idea what she was asking about.

"Your meeting with Simon," clarified Melissa, reading the confusion on his face.

The meeting had been a week ago now and James had thought he'd kept it from Melissa, not wanting to add to her burden in any way. He tried to stay neutral and not express any surprise or confusion. He also tried not to make it obvious that he were checking Melissa out to see where she was coming from with her question. Attempting to hide that he was trying to establish whether this was the on-form Melissa or that he was interacting with the other Melissa. She could be initiating a conversation about a meeting that James had had years previously.

Second guessing this was a perilous pursuit, but it would not do to go off half-cocked and talk at crossed purposes.

He decided to open with what he regarded as safe territory and it was a genuine, heartfelt sentiment in the current circumstances.

"You were right about him all along," he told his wife.

The words weighed heavy and he himself felt weighed down. It was the end of an era and all the worse for being a needless ending. It never should have turned out like this and he couldn't see anything he could have done differently to have changed it, not unless he had either a time machine or was all seeing and all knowing. Even with the strange and fortuitous occurrence of a time machine coming into his possession, what was he to do? He'd considered this one night as he stared at the ceiling, sleep yet again eluding his racing mind. Anything he said would equate to the last supper, *one of you will betray me.* And of course, he had thought about that time machine before. Going back and spending more time with Melissa and enjoying what little time that they had together. If the time machine had really good forward settings, then he would take Melissa into the future and have her treated. Have her cured of this terrible curse. That made him wonder how far he would need to go into the future and whether those trial and error trips to find a time where dementia was cured would be futile.

How would it feel to know that dementia was never cured? Probably cancer with it. Extinguishing that hope would be a brutal moment, and just thinking about it hurt James. Everything seemed to hurt James now. Simon's betrayal had left him bruised and raw and he had nothing left in the tank when it came to resilience. If he was knocked, he would fall and he would just lay there. Putting one foot in front of the other was difficult enough, it felt like he was wearing one of those old fashioned deep sea diver's suits with the lead shoes and brass helmet. He felt it physically. If he had the energy to be frightened by this, he would be. That the mental aspects of a hard knock in life could manifest itself physically so he struggled to move through the world was something he'd never known was possible. It turned out that hope and positivity helped a person counteract gravity. Without it, movement was a struggle.

Life was a struggle.

James felt Melissa's arms slip around him while he sat slumped at the kitchen table. She held him and didn't speak. He wondered what he would say in the circumstances, knew that he would have an urge to say something, to fill the silence with a solution. This despite also knowing that sometimes what was needed was this. A hug and a listening ear. That well-meaning advice aimed at providing a solution to help someone you loved out of a bad place was not needed at this time. Maybe later, but not now.

James felt the merits of this approach. He relaxed and enjoyed the close proximity of his wife. Felt her warmth spreading through him.

Eventually, Melissa spoke, breathing the words directly into

James' ear, "he was always a bit of a twat."

James stiffened in her arms and moved so he could see her face, he hadn't expected those words, others yes, but not those particular words. She responded to his movements and loosened her hug so he could turn to face her. Her eyes twinkled mischievously and a smile played upon her lips.

James felt himself relax even more, "he was, wasn't he?"

Her smile was infectious and he couldn't help but smile back. Then they kissed, a gentle, tentative kiss that neither of them wanted to break away from, the kiss becoming more insistent and passionate, both of them quickly losing themselves in the moment and in each other.

\* \* \*

Later, James glanced at the bedroom floor and smiled. The prospect of picking up these clothes amused him. These clothes had been discarded for very good reason and it was a small price to pay for the very good reason that he and Melissa had been indulging in until only a few moments ago. He was laying on his back, Melissa was curled up next to him, head on his chest.

"He's done you a favour," she said out of the blue.

"How do you figure that one out?" asked James, he was coming to a similar conclusion, but hearing it said out loud was still strange and he wanted to understand Melissa's reasoning.

Melissa propped herself up on an elbow and looked down at him.

"When you were starting out, you thought you needed him..."

"I..."

Melissa gave him a warning look, silencing him, "That might, or might not have been the case." She gave him an appraising look, "let's put it this way, if Simon hadn't been available, you would have muddled along in any case. Yes, you might have brought someone on to give you a hand. In fact, you definitely would because did! You're adept at finding the right people for the job, filling gaps that you create and filling them with capable people who you encourage and support and enthuse. So OK, first time around, Simon gave you enough breathing space for you to discover this about yourself. Maybe he can take the credit for being the unwitting catalyst to you coming into your own, but you have to know now that it was you, and it was always you. Simon was largely a lucky passenger."

"Saying he's a passenger is a bit harsh," James couldn't help but defend Simon.

"Jimmy!" Melissa sometimes playfully called him Jimmy when she wanted to reign him in a little. It was a variation on a mother calling their child their full name, the child knew they were in all sorts of trouble when that happened, "take

224

a moment. Step back and *think!* You were his minder. You couldn't trust him to behave properly. No one else in your business was like that, quite the opposite in fact, you brought them on, trusting them from the start and making sure they knew you trusted them to go out and do a good job, that you wouldn't micro manage them."

Melissa laughed.

"What?" asked James.

"That was part of what made you work so well, you had no choice but to empower your staff because you were too busy babysitting your man-child best friend!"

"I..." the words died before they reached his lips.

Melissa watched as the thoughts were processed in James mind.

"There you go! I think he's got it!" grinned Melissa.

James mock scowled at her, he wasn't completely dim. Only, maybe he had been blind-sided in one part of his life...

"We all have our weak spots," said Melissa sympathetically, "well, when I say *we,* we both know that what I actually mean is *men.* Men were not paying attention when the human race was doing some of its evolving and they have a bit of catching up to do!"

"OK, OK, Ms Greer!" James smiled at his wife.

"Your weakness here was your unquestioning loyalty, Jimmy-Boy. I think you should maybe question it in future, because what about your loyalty to your staff?"

James nodded at this. He was well aware that he had compromised far too often and to the detriment of his staff. That Simon had held too much sway and the direction he was intent on going was not one that James would have chosen and at times he just couldn't agree with it.

"And to your wife," Melissa added this sombrely.

The atmosphere in the room stilled and James felt a leaden lump in his stomach. He could not mistake the meaning of Melissa's words.

"He..?" James could not help but ask, but found that he did not want to hear Melissa's reply.

"Made a pass at me," she said sadly, "more than once."

"The..." began James, struggling with his anger and so struggling to select one of the many expletives scrolling at lightening pace through his mind right now.

"Complete and utter twat," supplied Melissa.

"Amongst other things!" hissed James.

Melissa stroked his chest, placating and soothing him, "let's not let him ruin a moment more in our lives, James. He's history and he's done us a favour. When you start again, you will build bigger and better. You know what success looks like, you totally have this and better still, people know it. You have a reputation, not just with clients and in the industry, but also with skilled and talented people who, when they know you're back, will knock on your door and beg to be let in to be a part of what you build. Simon has made a big mistake. He wanted what you had, but he's not bright enough to understand that he can never have it."

James looked at Melissa uncertainly, "you really think I can do it?"

"No," Melissa was suddenly cold, and harsh, "I don't think you can."

James was shocked and uncertain, and then Melissa's expression softened, "I *know* you can do it. You've already proven that. The best is yet to come."

She slipped her hand downwards, "speaking of which..."

And they spent the rest of the afternoon making memories.

# 22

Even as James stormed from the care home, leaving behind him a mildly bewildered Helen, he knew that he was behaving badly. Childishly. He was in danger of being the person he'd accused Simon of being. What he was going to tell Helen next - if he had stayed that was – was that his actions were not entirely altruistic, that he was being selfish because he also believed in karma and were he not to at least try to do the right thing then karma would creep up behind him and bite him on the arse.

Besides, why make a bad situation worse?

Why waste his time focusing on the crap that Simon had caused?

When it came to his particular business, it was all about reputation. James, Simon and his new friends all knew that, so were James to fight them it would end up being a pyrrhic victory. James would burn everything, including all his bridges. He'd have nowhere to move on to. Not in that world anyway. And in having done that, he would risk being consumed in self-loathing at his own stupidity. Being dragged into a situation

with those loathsome new friends of Simon was the worst thing
he could have done.

Only, he'd managed to do something pretty bad in any case.
He'd suppressed all his feelings and his anger at Simon so well,
but when Helen had been forthright with him. When she'd
said the exact things he'd thought himself, he'd turned on her.
He'd projected his own bad feelings and self-doubt on her and
stormed out.

So much for him being the better man. In a weird way, it was
good to know that he was far from perfect. He suspected that
he was partially enjoying wallowing in the toxic mud of his
bad behaviour. Revelling in the crud, because this was who he
really was and he deserved to feel bad. Bad about himself and
bad about the really shite hand that life had dealt him.

And then James did what he had always done. He busied
himself with the tasks ahead. He cracked on. There was much
to be said for this. After all, the devil makes work for idle hands
and James knew only too well that when his mind idled he
ended up in places he really didn't want to be, and making his
way from those self-same places was notoriously difficult and
it got harder to leave the longer he tarried.

Being busy usually had the added benefit of moving things
along, it did the way James usually approached things anyway.
Sometimes though, being busy was an avoidance strategy. The
irony was that when this was the only strategy in play, there
was no other plan and as a result a person went around in cir-
cles, rudderless and worse still clueless as to the foolhardiness

of their pursuit. Because they were too busy to notice what they were really doing.

This was what James did this time around. He stayed busy and he ignored the bad situation he had left behind him, or rather, bad situations, one of which there was merit in leaving well alone. He would do well to let the dust settle on Simon and his former business. Clear his head, allow his emotions to calm and then think about his *what next*. A what next that entailed starting again and building an even better business that would emerge in the same space as Simon's and take large chunks out of it and more importantly, allow his former employees the option to work with him again and enjoy their work lives once more.

He would wait. Then, if Simon and his chums had any further tricks up their sleeves, such as claiming he had a restraint of trade clause (which he most definitely didn't) the time elapsed would make all of that go away. It would be a fresh start. James would start all over again.

The horrible truth of it all was that he knew what this really meant.

He would start over again without Melissa. The bare bones of his plan entailed emerging from this part of his life, burying his wife and starting all over again in the biggest and most terrible way he could imagine.

Alone.

He was not going to help himself on that score if he was going to act like a complete dick when he was hurt. Taking things out on someone who had been kind and leant him support and a listening ear when he most needed it was ridiculously stupid, and of course James knew this. Knowing it did not help though. He'd somehow painted himself into a corner, or had done so as far as he was concerned. It didn't matter what anyone else thought, this was all about him and his ego and his pride.

And so he left it to fester. He allowed himself to be pig-headed and to make his life harder when it was already at the hardest it had ever been.

* * *

Life got harder.

Life did its thing and it was as though it had heard James think that things were the hardest they had ever been, it taught James that whenever he thought he'd reached the hardest point or that things were now at rock bottom there was always the possibility of harder and of lower and when those things came James just had to deal with them. Or not. It was about surviving. Weathering the storms. There were dramatic moments, but mostly things crept up on him. It was like he was in a sealed and pressurised environment and some dispassionate being was slowly turning the dial up such that the pressure kept increasing. Testing him. Seeing just how much he could take.

The problem was that James hadn't been able to take any more for some time now. He had been running on empty and didn't know what to do about it. Just as he thought he'd hit a wall and couldn't take anymore he realised he was somehow still going.

The bitter-sweet oases of normality kept him going. There were good times with Melissa, albeit, they were both haunted by the disease. It cast a permanent shadow now, and neither of them could ignore it. No longer could they pretend that it wasn't there, at least for a while. All holidays were cancelled and they lived with the dark thing in their lives twenty four seven.

Help came daily, but provided little respite for James. There were always things to do, even with the help, and he had gotten to a point where he couldn't leave Melissa. The carer assured him that he could, but she didn't understand. James needed to be there. He'd made a promise and now Melissa needed him more than she ever had. Leaving her even for a moment felt completely and utterly wrong to him.

He never once stopped to think that maybe it was his need he was fulfilling, or that that was at least a part of it now, that he was clinging on to her in the vain hope that he could arrest the progress of this terrible disease and keep her with him always. He frequently imagined what it must be like for Melissa. It hurt him to revisit his inability to truly empathise with her now. In the worst possible way, she was trapped and alone, fighting a losing battle, knowing that she was always going to lose. He knew he couldn't fully know or appreciate her plight and that added to his burden. He felt like he was failing her.

## 22

All James could do was understand that whatever he was going through, however broken and empty he felt, it was nothing when compared to what his wife was going through and so he had to carry on, come what may. This stoic and hard view of life meant that he was failing to look after himself.

It never occurred to him that he may have pushed Helen away when he did because he knew that all of this was coming. That he had purposely isolated himself. Shutting himself off completely from the outside world so his total focus was on Melissa.

It seemed a damaging thing to do. To shun help and support. And it was. James' way of coping was not to cope and instead to adopt a form of self-pitying martyrdom, to slowly self-destruct alongside his dying wife. Deep down, he could see this was wrong, that he was emulating his Granddad, but he could see no other way. In his own way, he was as trapped as Melissa was and he could see no way out.

# 23

They made hay whenever the sun shone.

Despite the downward spiral into the confines of a world which pressed in upon them on all sides, they made the most of their time together. If anyone was to capture any of these moments, they would see why James was loathed to leave Melissa's side. It was these moments that he lived for. This was when Melissa lit up and James always had pen and paper to hand to note down her memories, to listen and to encourage her to explore her recollections.

These sessions now took place curled up on the sofa, or in bed. Melissa was most comfortable in these spots and invariably fell asleep before the end. James had a series of unfinished recollections, but had not once attempted to revisit them in an attempt to establish a suitable ending. If Melissa repeated herself and recounted a memory James had already recorded he said not a word and instead faithfully put pen to paper and listened to her intently as he did so.

He noticed that she was falling asleep sooner and sooner and it was when she covered the same ground that he really saw the difference in her. He could see the decline and the rate of it and it worried him.

Today, as they sat on the sofa, they were camping near Ambleside. The *they* of it were Melissa's college friends. Girls together in the first couple of weeks of the summer holidays. Spending time together at the end of college and before their lives would be taken up with work and everything that went along with that. A last hurrah before reality really set in. An end to an era and the delaying of the start of the rest of their lives and challenges that, when they looked back, they would never be ready for. Nothing prepared you for the life outside of childhood and at the time, they were full of vim, vigour and a sense that the world was at their feet. That they had arrived and it was just a case of taking their places at the table.

There was something Enid Blyton about the stories Melissa was telling of this time. There were walks and picnics and time spent in the great outdoors adventuring. Everything was done on a shoe string as none of them had any money, so they did everything on a budget. Cheese sandwiches sat on a hill were a lot cheaper than a meal in a pub, and as the weather was kind, they had the best of it.

The weather in The Lakes is fickle at the best of times. That entire region of Britain is infamous for its rain with Manchester, Lancaster and The Lakes battling it out as the rainiest of locations. The two weeks they spent in The Lakes were some of the hottest that they had known, dare they say it, *too hot.* Too hot for walking in and too hot to lay under canvas in June when the nights are at their shortest. The sun would be up bright and early and by 5am, it had been baking the canvas of the tent and the occupants inside for a good hour.

They were young and care free and sleep was for losers as far as they were concerned, so none of them tried to compensate for lack of sleep by turning in early that evening. Besides, the sun stuck around until after ten and all that daylight enlivened them. There were others of their kind on the camp site and after the first day they clustered together drinking cheap booze, listening to music and talking loudly, laughing even louder. This did not make them popular with certain other elements of the campsite and after a few days, they made a coordinated effort to up pitches and make a corner of the farmer's field the Exciting Corner.

The excitement was all good clean fun, or at least was if Melissa was to be believed. James sometimes wondered whether Melissa's recounting of her past was edited and sanitised so as to appeal to as wide an audience as possible. Was an autobiography really a representative account of someone's life, or was it the story according to them and what they would like you to think of them? Never mind that, was it a form of editing for their personal edification? Was this what everyone did? Replay parts of their lives and tweak the edit so it was more favourable? More palatable for them personally? After all, we all have to look in the mirror and live with ourselves, so there must be a drive to change the story and make it softer and more appealing. All this spin done by the softer and more appealing self.

It wasn't as though James wanted a warts and all account.

James was all too aware of this. He had an idea of who Melissa was, so if she had launched into an account of her life on the wrong side of the tracks. Mistreated by alcoholic parents, fighting from the age of five in underground child fighting rings, progressing to the barbaric so-called sport of animal fighting, starting with a cage full of angry hamsters and progressing to larger and more fearsome animals as her reputation grew in tandem with her appetite for ultra-violence. A life of violent, hedonistic narcissism that she had left at the door of the pub on the night she had met James, making him wait a full six months before he could see an inch of the flesh she concealed almost totally, as she had all of her prison tattoos lasered away.

We all have a dark side and a few stories we may not wish to tell, James was well aware of one of those stories of Melissa's. It sat in a box, somewhere in their home. Maybe that was everything. Her dark, secret side in its totality, but did it speak of other secrets, more darkness and a life lived that Melissa was keeping under wraps?

Those two weeks Melissa had spent in The Lakes with her college friends had been idyllic. There had been fun and silliness and Melissa confessed to some kissing. *Some kissing.* When James repeated the phrase with a view to having it expanded and explained, Melissa smiled.

"A girl has to have her secrets!"

James eyed his wife. He wrote, *there was some kissing,* resisting the urge to churlishly drop *indiscriminate* down there on the page. Melissa was either intimating things that may or may not have happened, or enjoying the poor concealment of her having kissed other women. This, she knew, was a well-publicised fantasy for men. She also knew that, men may well talk a good game when it came to this sort of thing, but when it actually happened, they could behave very differently. Mostly people had a solid world view and they did not thank you kindly when you shook it up and introduced anything that didn't fit their careful constructions.

Of course, that was then and this was now, and could anyone truly see something as it had been without altering it via the view they had of the world today? That was another reason for the careful construction of a story. It had to make *sense* in the here and now.

There had been one particularly late night towards the end of the holiday. It wasn't a late night for all. In ones and twos, people had peeled off and taken to their beds. Some had actually slept.

In the end, there were four of them left, Melissa, her friend Jane and two lads from a small town near Manchester, Melissa couldn't remember where exactly, wasn't sure she'd been paying attention when they said, if they had said. They had the accents though and they were nice guys. Boys next door, verging on nerdy.

Jane and Melissa were attempting to drink the cheap, super-market gin they had bought the previous day. This was before the gin revolution, when the popularity of gin soared and hundreds of variations on the drink hit the market. This gin was rough around the edges and seemed to get rougher as they drank it. Their determination not to be beaten by the bottle of firewater increased as they drank more and it's taste worsened. Steve, one of the boys, suggested putting the gin in tea to take the edge off. At first, this seemed like a silly idea and neither of the girls took it seriously, but as they looked at their empty glasses and considered the prospect of another onslaught, they revisited the gin tea idea.

"Isn't it going to taste vile with PG Tips?" asked Jane.

Steve laughed, "I didn't mean normal tea!"

Jane looked confused.

"Don't you have any herbal tea? Mint tea maybe?"

Both of the girls now frowned at Steve, did they look like herbal tea drinkers? These were simpler times and this was also before the surge in the popularity of herbal teas.

"Steve has some," said Gary helpfully, "why don't you grab some, mate?"

Steve seemed to eye his friend suspiciously, almost as though Gary was using this as a ploy to whisk both girls away from under his nose, not that he really had a chance with either of them, he wasn't their type. Gary might have been, but events had moved on beyond that sort of thing now and they all knew that. It would have ruined things if either Gary or Steve made a move. Of course, if Melissa or Jane had made a move, the lads were unlikely to find a reserve of chivalry and gently, but firmly rebuff their advances. Melissa wasn't sure whether she knew that at the time, possibly not.

Steve took his time getting up and taking his leave in order to locate his stash of herbal tea and return with it, it turned out that Steve's glaring at his mate was largely because he was good and comfortable and begrudged having to move away from his spot. Once he was up though, he was off and back in what seemed a matter of seconds, the passing of time distorted by the night, their laughter and the drink they had already consumed.

There were a selection of tea bags.

"His Mum bought them for him, said if we were camping, herbal tea was an absolute must. It turns out that she was right, eh!" quipped Gary.

Steve didn't seem to appreciate mention of his Mum, and was obviously needled by Gary's mention of her. Or it could have been that he was embarrassed that she had foisted uncool tea bags upon him and that this did not paint him in the best of lights. He handed the boxes of tea bags to Melissa and Jane and asked which they would like. None of the tea bags stood out and the girls fell into a puddle of indecision that threatened to consume the remainder of the night.

"Why don't we put one of each in the pot?" suggested Gary.

"We?" challenged Jane.

"Well, I thought we'd help you over the finish line?" explained Gary, now on uncertain ground.

Jane eyed him wearily and said nothing, instead she busied herself with the brewing of the tea, following Gary's suggestion of a mix of herbal bags.

"Don't put the gin in until the end, you don't want to boil the alcohol off," said Steve when it looked like Jane was going to add the remainder of the gin to the near boiling water.

"As if I would do that," said Jane sternly, lowering the bottle from her pending emptying of the rest of the bottle into the boiling liquid.

Tea brewed and taken off the heat, Jane was about to add the gin. She seemed to be in a rush when it came to emptying that bottle.

"Hang on, let's taste the tea first," Melissa suggested, "although... I'm not sure whether it matters whether it tastes good or not, it certainly won't when we add that bloody gin!"

They all did a taste test.

"Interesting," said Jane having taken a slurp of the hot, herby liquid.

It was indeed interesting, not terribly bad, but also not something that any of them would be recommending or attempting to replicate any time soon. They knew this even in their inebriated state.

"Now comes the moment of truth!" exclaimed Jane and now there was certainly no stopping her as she emptied the entire contents of the bottle into the tea.

"Can we at least try a bit?" asked Gary.

Melissa laughed, "we should have let them try the gin first – so they knew what all the fuss was about."

Jane shrugged, that horse had bolted. She poured a splash into two tin mugs. The white tin mugs with blue edging that were compulsory camping accessories once upon a time. She handed them to the lads and waited expectantly.

"Go on then!" she chided.

The lads looked at each other, seeming to regret having asked for a taste, and wrong footed by the absence of gin tea in the girls' hands. They reached a silent conclusion and as one, they drank the sample in one go.

"Savour it, boys!" giggled Melissa as she saw them attempt to down the liquid in one go.

They did as they were bade and the girls fell into paroxysms of laughter at the sight of the two boys. Their faces contorting with the effort of drinking the gin tea. They would have won international gurning competitions with those faces, a joint victory as there was nothing to separate the comedy rictus expressions on both of their countenances.

"Oy! Keep it down! Some of us are trying to sleep!" shouted a man across the camping site.

His shouting woke up half the sight and the four revellers helped matters by following his shouting with a series of shushes that carried across the night air.

"Stop that bloody shushing!" shouted the same man.

"Stop that bloody shouting!" screamed a woman.

All four of the late night crew collapsed into fits of laughter, made all the more difficult to break out of as they attempted to supress any noise from said laughter. They were all back in class and feeling like the most wonderfully naughty children. Melissa remembered the feeling of light headed giddiness, the elation of letting go and having simple fun. That was a part of why this was such a good memory for her.

Jane was the first to regain some semblance of composure. By the time the lads had followed suit they were being handed mugs full of the tea. When shared between the four of them, the last of the gin was all gone bar the shouting and there would be no more shouting this night. They'd been warned on that score.

"I thought..." began Gary.

"You've earnt it," winked Jane.

Melissa snorted a laugh behind her mug, what Jane meant was that, having seen the boy's reaction to the vile liquid they'd been made to drink, she had made an executive decision which amounted to a problem shared...

They all girded their loins and watched each other over the rims of their mugs. None of them wanting to go first, all of them wanting to jump in together. Not trusting the other three to uphold their part of the drinking bargain.

"After two?" suggested Melissa.

The others nodded grimly.

"One..." began Melissa.

"Hold on, do we go on two or after two?" asked Gary, ever the practical one apparently.

"You what?" asked Melissa.

James could imagine that confrontational *you what* very well, Melissa could be brusque and forthright at times.

"I mean," said Gary, "we could either drink as you say *two*, or you may intend to count to two and then say, *go?*"

"Ah, right," said Melissa.

23

"Let's just drink on two then, eh?"

Gary nodded for all of them.

"Ready?" asked Melissa.

More grim nodding.

"Two!" cried Melissa.

And she drank. Thankfully the mugs were cold and had reduced the temperature of the liquid, as had the addition of the gin and also the time elapsed with fits of giggles and shouted tellings off.

Melissa went at it like a good un and drank for all she was worth.

Jane found her approach to the start hilarious, but had managed to valiantly commence her attempt at drinking the foul tea, but then she failed in a fit of wet giggles, a spout of herbal liquid hit Steve square in the face and he froze, agog at this development.

They all fell into another bout of uncontrollable laughter which did nothing to ingratiate them to the other campers, so they decided they should leave for somewhere more suitable.

"Shall we take our tea with us?" asked Steve.

Melissa raised her own mug and slowly and theatrically up-

245

ended it. One drop of liquid hung to the mug's edge for a moment before letting go and falling to the grass.

"Shit!" said Gary in admiration.

Melissa had downed her brew in a oner.

The other three looked down despondently at their near full mugs. They would bring them with.

"Where are we going?" asked Jane as they exited the campsite and turned left.

Walking in the dark along the deserted lane.

The dark was the magical blue light of a June Summer. On certain nights, when the sky was clear, it never really got properly dark, instead a blue filter transformed the landscape. It was wonderful and no doubt had all four of them vowing to stay awake more often so they could enjoy not only the beauty of nights like this, but to do so away from the rest of humanity, for no one else was up and about at this time of night.

"Let's go up there," suggest Gary.

No one actually saw where Gary was pointing, but they all liked his suggestion of *up there.*

"And once we're up there?" asked Jane.

"Let's watch the sun rise," Steve said this and he said it

breathlessly. There was an endearing, childlike quality to the way he said it and it was a fine suggestion. A great way to round the night off.

None of them thought beyond that moment and the consequences of having had no sleep and the prospect of no sleep until the following night as the tents during the baking hot Summer's days were uninhabitable.

Not long into the walk, as they left the last vestiges of civilisation and found themselves out in the countryside of the Lakes, Steve, aided and abetted by the drink he'd consumed and in particular the mug of gin tea, upped his pace and left the other three behind. They watched as he walked into the middle of the road and lay there, staring up into the sky with wide eyes.

"I fucking love this place!" he shouted up to the stars.

The other three chuckled and glanced down at him as they carried on walking. Five minutes later, they seemed to realise they were a man down.

"Do you think he's still laying in the middle of the road?" asked Melissa.

"Nah, Steve's Captain Sensible, he'll..." Gary trailed off, not convinced by his own words, "I'd best go and check on him hadn't I?" it sounded like a suggestion, but he'd already broken into a jog back down the road. Lying in a road, in the dark, even if the dark wasn't properly dark was a really dangerous thing to do. There were probably farmers and gamekeepers who were out at this time and they wouldn't expect a drunken lad to be laying in the road, would probably not even slow their Land Rover as they bore down upon Steve.

Melissa and Jane carried on walking. Melissa questioned why it was that they didn't stop, it didn't seem an option at the time, but they did listen out for the two lads and they could hear first Gary and then mumbling from Steve, then grumbling from Steve and then some light bickering that increased in volume as the lads caught up with the girls.

They carried on with their walk and despite the gin, that they had all polished off early on in their walk, they began to sober up and as they sobered up, their energy dwindled and as they tired, their appetite for the walk ebbed away.

"Nearly there!" said Gary with false cheer.

"I've never seen a sun rise from a hill in the Lakes," said Melissa.

And they all chipped in with encouraging words, needing them as much for themselves as the others.

As they neared the top of the hill, they fell into silence and all they could hear was the sound of their laboured breathing and their footsteps disturbing the scree on the path.

"We should have brought some water with us," said Melissa as they all found a seat on the rocks atop the hill. She instantly regretted introducing the concept of thirst, but it was said now and there was no going back.

They sat.

That was when it all changed. They sat, glad of the rest and the silence and peace of the mountain soaked into them.

Or at least it began to, Gary sighed a loud sigh of contentment, "this is great in't it?"

He was greeted with silence in response. He nodded imperceptibly as he realised what was required of him. No one was to pollute the stillness of the occasion. They had arrived and this was it. There was nothing to say, it was all about soaking up the moment and enjoying it for what it was.

"Some would say it was the simplicity of the moment," said Melissa, "but I think that would be missing something important. There is nothing simple about nature, is there? It was wonderful and awe inspiring and a rare moment for a person to really take stock. I felt so small in that moment as I got how fleeting and inconsequential my existence really was. That I was less than a blink of an eye in this place. But at the same time, I felt so alive and lucky to have this life and to have this moment. This was what life was all about. Never taking for granted what you have before you. Taking the time to take it in and to be truly thankful for it. I think I saw God in that moment, James. I *understood*."

James remained silent, he had never seen Melissa like this. So animated. So alive. It was wonderful, but also terrible in its finality, she was looking back and would never look forward again. Not like this.

Melissa burst out laughing.

The suddenness of it was shocking and so out of kilter with what she had been saying that it shocked James. He felt like he'd been rudely awakened.

"Then Gary pointed out that it was light. 'It's light,' he said, 'when did it get light'. Then it dawned on us that it had already dawned on us! We all turned around, feeling the warmth of the sun on our backs, it had only crept up behind us as we sat there and none of us had noticed!"

James smiled.

"That added to the moment somehow, that we thought we were so clever and yet we failed at something so simple." Melissa seemed to sober as her mind was cast back over the years, she looked up, her eyes brimming with tears, "I've never seen the sun rise in The Lakes."

James reached out to her and she collapsed into his arms and sobbed.

# 24

Later, they were curled up in bed together.

James reflected upon the day, it hadn't been a bad one. It had had its moments, but more often than not, Melissa had been lucid and today she had recounted an entire memory. There was less of that happening these days, so James would take that and then some.

Melissa's breathing was regular, slow and heavy and he assumed that she was asleep until she spoke.

"I've been thinking..." she began.

"Oh dear..." James responded automatically with his stock answer, then realised that it been some while since she'd admitted to a bout of thinking.

She leant back and play punched his arm before resettling with her head on his chest.

"I like hearing your heartbeat when we're like this," she told him.

251

"That was what you were thinking?" he asked her, knowing that it was an unlikely answer, but saying it all the same.

"No," she said firmly and seriously, "I've been thinking about our conversations. I should really have thought about this and talked to you before now."

"Yes...?" he said warily, wondering if she was going to spill the beans on her former life.

"Well, you know if you carry on with all this talking to me, it'll just make it more difficult for you to move on and to find someone else? There's something to be said about making your own person and superimposing it on an innocent victim – it's quite portable that one..."

She was talking into his chest, he craned his neck to look at her, but barring the top of her head he could not see her and definitely couldn't gauge her expression.

"Where's this come from?" he asked her.

"Do you really want me to answer that?" she said it light-heartedly, but it still contained an edge to it.

"I suppose not," he agreed, "I just don't want you talking like this."

Now she got up and propped herself on her elbow so she was looking at him, "we do have to talk, Jimmy-boy. It would be sad if we didn't. And right now, I can talk. So I am. We neither of us know how much more of this we have left."

James sighed, she was right, but it was horrible hearing it. He felt like some sort of accountant at times, a dark and terrible sort with absolutely no humanity, because what he was doing was looking at the numbers and forecasting their future. Playing the percentages to see where the tipping point was. When would there be too much of the disease and not enough of his Melissa? Would he even spot her in amongst the episodes and the chaos? Or would he be so embroiled in trying to survive and so exhausted with the effort that he couldn't see her anymore?

"I want you to be happy. You're young and you're a good bloke. Just don't..." she began.

"What?" he asked, and when she wasn't forthcoming, "come on, you can't leave it like that!"

She looked at him curiously, "don't do that thing that some people do."

"Which is!?"

"Attempting to find a doppelgänger of the person they lost. Because there isn't one, OK? You need to go for someone... *different.*"

"OK, like who?" asked James.

The conversation was odd, but not as bad as it could have been, mostly because James wasn't taking it at all seriously. He just couldn't think of a future without Melissa right now, let alone letting someone else into his life. James was now curious though. He found that he wanted Melissa's take on this. She knew him. If she was going to do some matchmaking, what would her input be? He wondered whether he would concur with her take on things, or baulk at her suggested match. He was already convinced it would be the latter, whatever she suggested.

She shrugged, "dunno," was all she said.

"You can be a right bugger at times!" said an exasperated James, "why bring it up and then leave it all hanging!?"

She shrugged again and grinned at him.

"OK," he said, having had a brainwave, "which three celebrities would you send me on a date with?"

"Ooh! Good one!" she beamed, "you go first!"

"Ahhh! Why do you always do that!"

She grinned again, then nodded at him, "go on, who would you send me on dates with, with a view to me finding my next husband?"

"It's weird when you say it like that..." said James, suddenly serious again.

"I know..." she said sadly, then she brightened again, "but come on! Play the game!"

James rolled his eyes, "Thor," he said as his opener.

"Chris Hemsworth?" asked Melissa.

"Yes, but as Thor, I wouldn't set you up with him if he was the character in the Ghostbusters reboot."

"Ah, OK. I like that added dimension." She frowned, "I'm not sure that counts as one of the three, wouldn't he be my pre-date?"

"What do you mean?"

"You know, bit of a fling to get me back in the game? Bit of fun with that big hammer of his and..."

"Alright, alright! Stop right there! So you like the packaging, but he's not a long term prospect. I get that now!"

"Yup, so who else?"

"This is difficult!" groaned James.

"No one said it would be easy!"

"Right, I'm going to come up with another bloke and then you have to come up with your first date for me. We'll alternate."

"Oh, OK then..." she agreed grudgingly.

"Bruce Banner," said James.

"Are you setting me up exclusively with heroes?" exclaimed Melissa.

"Nothing but the best for you, dear!" smiled James.

"I think you should spread your net wider with the next one, no more comic book characters, OK?"

James nodded, "killjoy... You know I'm onto a winner and you've not poo-pooed Bruce, so he's a potential suitor, with his quiet ways and deep intellect. Quite like me, really, only I don't have a green alter-ego when I get angry."

"You tried that, and it didn't work out, remember?"

"Wha...?"

James was fractionally slow on the uptake, then the penny dropped. She meant Simon. James rolled his eyes, she wasn't far off the mark there and that was a very sharp quip. He suppressed a shudder as the pending loss of that wit and intellect struck him.

"You OK?" she asked him.

"Yes... cat walked over my grave," he said without thinking.

256

She frowned. He wasn't sure exactly what she was frowning at, but wanted to move quickly on, "so, who are you going to send me on a date with?"

"Kate Winslet," said Melissa with conviction.

"Oh, OK..." James wasn't convinced with this choice, thought maybe she was a little too...

"When she was in Extras," added Melissa mischievously.

"Oh!" smiled James.

Winslet had shown another side to her in Extras and had played up to Ricky Gervais in quite an open and in your face way.

"I thought we weren't to choose people who were too alike to us?"

"What do you mean?" asked Melissa, not seeing the comparison between herself and Kate Winslet.

"Well, in Extras, she was really dirty!"

Melissa mimed slapping him, "cheeky bugger!"

He grinned.

"Go one then?" he prompted for his next match.

"Oy! It's your turn," she protested.

"Worth a try," he winked, "OK... can we pick actors living or dead and choose their age and era?"

"Yeah, go on then..." agreed Melissa.

"Bob Mortimer when he was forty," said James.

"Bob..." Melissa looked set to protest, but now she was thinking about it and the frown that had beset her face softened and then she eventually smiled, "oh! Good one! He's lovely isn't he?"

"Seems like a genuine bloke, *and* he's really funny. Funnier than you. I think you'd get on like a house on fire."

"We would," she agreed, "good job I didn't meet him before you came along or you'd have missed out!"

"I wouldn't have blamed you for running off with him if he'd come along after we met..." smiled James.

"My celebrity pass? That's not a bad call," nodded Melissa.

"Yes, although strictly speaking, celebrity passes are a licence to have a one off bunk up with someone famous aren't they?"

"Yeah..." said Melissa, "and so far you've chosen my celebrity pass bunk up and my celebrity pass run away with and start a new life, can't wait to see where you go with your third choice!"

"No pressure then!" chuckled James, "you're turn!"

258

4

"Hmmm, this isn't as easy as I thought it would be. There are plenty of nice and likeable celebs, but would I want them in my home, canoodling with you on my sofa?"

"That's... I... can we move on from that thought, please?!" whined James.

"Yes, sorry... I'm getting a bit carried away with the detail here aren't I?"

"You are, I had a mental image of you fishing with Bob, thank you very much. Let's keep it at that level!"

"OK..." agreed Melissa, but she couldn't help adding, "... prude!"

James rolled his eyes, "so as well as Kate Winslet, you'd set me up on a date with?"

"Katherine Ryan," stated Melissa with the same conviction as she had delivered Kate Winslet to James.

James scrunched his face up, he knew the name, but couldn't quite place it...

"Canadian? Comedian? Eight out of..." prompted Melissa.

"Oh! Right!" nodded James, now he had it, "why?"

"Erm, funny, feisty, wouldn't take any nonsense, and would bring a top level canoodling game to the sofa!"

259

"Oy! I thought we said we weren't going there!?"

"You did, yes."

"Right, anyway. Good choice and fine reasoning. I think you're still sailing close to someone like you?"

"Nah...! Really?" she was checking James out to see if he was being serious.

"Yes, really," he counted off on his fingers, "Funny, feisty, doesn't take any crap, top level canoodling game..."

She smiled a certain smile, "really?" she breathed, before kissing him.

The kiss led to a prolonged interruption to their conversation...

* * *

Afterwards, as they snuggled up again, Melissa picked up where they had left.

"So, who's my third date then?"

"Are we back on this again?" James said it like he really didn't want to resume the conversation and complete the list, but Melissa knew different. She read something in the way he spoke that assured her they would pick their final celebrity dates.

"We are, choose wisely padawan!" she said in a Yoda voice.

"So you've had Thor as an appetizer, then the Hulk and then Bob, so who would you round off with..?" James rubbed his chin thoughtfully with his free hand.

He went through star after star, dismissing them for what were probably spurious reasons, this was more difficult than it had at first seemed, or at least it was if you were doing it right. He was sure he was overlooking some ideal candidates too.

"Got it!" he at last exclaimed, "only... I had no candidates, and wouldn't you know it, three have come along at once, so you'd have to choose from the following three..."

"Ooh! I like that! But don't expect the same treatment, buster!"

"They are, in no particular order, David Coulthard, Steve Jones and Adam Driver."

"Steve Jones, David's Formula One co-presenter?" asked Melissa.

"Yeah," confirmed James.

"That could be awkward!" laughed Melissa.

"They're both good blokes though and I couldn't choose between the two of them!"

"What if I couldn't?" asked Melissa.

"No! Don't go there!"

She chuckled, "and you only picked Adam because I did the Yoda voice!

"Did not," refuted James.

"Did so," disagreed Melissa.

"OK, you might have helped lead me there, although I started with Keanu and for some reason I thought Adam was a bit more... you?"

"OK, I'd have Keanu as my celebrity pass then," decided Melissa as though this was all real and she was going ahead with it.

"Right... so you're dumping Thor from that spot..." said James, "anyway, who's my third date then?"

"Well," said Melissa, "you've had some dirt and you've had some laughs. Times two really, so that can only mean..."

She grinned at him in a particularly mischievous manner.

"Oh Lordy!" cried James.

"Well, it's wildcard time and you picked a wildcard with Bob Mortimer, so..."

"Hit me..." sighed James.

"Bjork!" announced Melissa gleefully.

"Bjork? But she's..." James trailed off.

"She's?" asked Melissa.

"I don't know what she is!" said James.

"Good," said Melissa.

"Good? How's that good?"

"Well, I'm one of a kind and so is Bjork. She'll give you plenty to think about won't she?"

"Hang on, you're making it sound like you've written off Kate and Katherine and I'm marrying Bjork come what may?!"

"Yup, sorry girls, I'm afraid you were no match for the force of nature that is Bjork," she smiled warmly at her husband, "just you take care of her, OK? She isn't as tough as she tries to make out."

"Now you're scaring me," James was doing things with his eyebrows as he tried to suss his wife out, "you're acting like you know her and you're also acting like this is a done deal."

Melissa shrugged and then snuggled back down on his chest. She said something he didn't quite catch.

"What was that?"

She repeated it even more quietly. It sounded like, *maybe it is, maybe it isn't.* James would never know because now Melissa was fast asleep.

What she had actually said as she was drifting off was...

*...Possibly Maybe.*

# 25

"I don't know how you do it?"

Helen looked up from rolling her cigarette, "years of practice," she said holding the cigarette out between them.

James thought about it, decided that although he didn't actually want the cigarette, he should take it. It was a kind of reverse peace offering. He was the one who should have been holding out a peace offering, he knew that only too well, but as Helen had beaten him to the punch, it was for him to take the proffered cigarette.

Helen began rolling a second cigarette.

"Not that," James nodded towards her industrious fingers, "this, *being* a carer."

Helen finished rolling the cigarette, then looked up at James, "you know what, for such a bright bloke, you can be such an idiot," she sighed and put her cigarette to her mouth. Lit it, then lit his cigarette.

James drew on the rollie, pleased that he didn't cough his guts up, conscious that this may mean that he was on the road to addiction to a substance that would end up killing him.

Helen shook her head at James, "you got my note then?"

"Yes. I..." he shrugged, "thank you." They were the only words that would do right now.

Helen had been past James house several times. She'd even stopped outside and thought about knocking, but each and every time her courage had deserted her. She convinced herself that it was a bad idea and that she would be encroaching upon James' personal space and disregarding his wishes, if he'd wanted to see her then he would have come to the care home. That was their arrangement and there was nothing beyond that.

Eventually, she had gotten over herself. She knew that James was in a bad place and that there was no harm in her dropping him a note to remind him that she was there. She'd even bought a card when she was next shopping, but then put it to one side, thinking it was too much. She tried to write the note itself several times. Scrunching it up and binning it even before she reread it, the words painful and stilted.

What should she write?

She was all too aware that she had been critical of the man and picked him up on his own words when he was being a bit up himself. As she saw her own written words she realised that she was just as bad. Words came so easily most of the time, but sometimes, when it really counted, they absented themselves and those that you could find missed the mark or risked making matters worse. What she really wanted to provide was an open door to sympathy and support. There was nothing she could say that would make it better, that was what she saw in the cold light of day. She couldn't let James remain isolated though. Not on her account anyway.

In the end, she had settled on something simple and light-hearted.

*Fancy a brew? H*

It was an invitation.

It made darn sure that James knew the door was open and better still the kettle was on and he was assured of a warm welcome. She never signed her name with an initial. Somehow it seemed right though. And that was even before she thought about the eventuality of Melissa picking the note up. Helen didn't want a confused Melissa asking who the hell Helen was. If she was in a state at finding a note on the door mat, then James could explain H a lot more easily than Helen. Not that there was anything to explain away, but dementia didn't care about the rights and wrongs of the real world, it created its own rights and wrongs and they defied logic even more than the outside world did, which was saying something.

They smoked their cigarettes and shared a companionable silence. That quiet time let both of them get used to each other again and dispel any worry-born nonsense. There was friendship here and it had always been here. Nothing had changed on that front and it was something both of them valued.

It was also something James sorely needed, but that was not to say that Helen didn't need it too. Friendship is a two way street and there is something for everyone when it is done right.

"How do I do this?" Helen was repeating the question, asking James if this was really what he wanted an answer to.

He did, "yes," he said firmly, "how do you keep going."

She pulled on the last of her cigarette, "do you want that brew?" she asked him.

He nodded, had another go on his rollie, dropping it and crushing it under foot before following her.

Inside, she handed him a brew and then sat opposite him, "it's different, what I do."

"How so?" asked James.

"Well, d'oh!" chuckled Helen, "I don't live here. This is not my home. So, in that respect, I have help and support and I can go home and recharge my batteries."

James nodded. He felt a bit silly asking now. It was bleeding obvious the difference between where he was and what Helen did, but still, Helen's life was closer to his than anyone else he knew and if anyone was going to get it, she was.

"OK, but how do you find the strength to go on?"

Helen looked askance at him.

"You're not telling me that you don't find this difficult?" he said.

She nodded, then made a show of thinking about it, "OK, just remember that it's different for me, OK?"

James nodded.

"I didn't set out to work in care homes, I tried a few other things first. Hairdresser for one."

"I can see you as a hairdresser," said James.

She eyed him suspiciously, "I don't know whether that's a good or a bad thing," she said.

He shrugged, neither did he.

"Anyway, I don't think I was cut out for it..."

"Ah, I see what you did there!" smiled James.

Helen scowled, then it dawned on her what he meant, "Oh do shut up!" but she chuckled as she said this, "I found myself in a care home one day. I wouldn't say I chose it. It didn't choose me either. I needed the work and I got on with it. Do you remember your first days in work?" she asked him earnestly.

James thought back, "vaguely. I was a rabbit in the headlights. Mostly it's alien to who I am now though. It's like when you go to a primary school and you see the seats. You know you must have sat in them, but knowing that you did doesn't help you see it any more clearly, does it? It doesn't compute! I was never that small!!"

Helen nodded, "well my first days and weeks and months and maybe even years were like that. I became a different person. I bloody well grew up was what happened!" she laughed.

James smiled.

"I've learnt to deal with it, mate. Part of that is loving and respecting these people, but more importantly making sure that I like them. Whatever happens, whatever they do. I make darn sure that I like them. And If I find myself slipping, then I work out what I need to do. I'm responsible for each and every one of them, but I'm also responsible for me. So I behave and I look after myself too. Because if I don't look after myself then I'll get tired and stressed and it's when I'm at my worst that I'm really at my worst, if you know what I mean?"

James nodded, he knew exactly what she meant.

"Have you got anyone?" asked Helen.

James began to react, thought Helen was asking if he was up to no good, his beleaguered mind not going where it should quickly enough. He shook his head to clear it, "we have a cleaner who is kind of a friend, that helps. We also get these fifteen minute visits a few times a day. That's what the state provides and it's a bit of help, but it's over before it's begun and it's nearly as disruptive as it is helpful..." he trailed off.

"Difficult having people come in, isn't it?" said Helen.

James almost bridled, wanted to ask her how the hell she would know. Saw something in her face.

"Did you do call outs? Home care?" he asked instead.

She nodded, "for a while, yes. Then I came back to this."

"So you've seen it from the other side."

She nodded again, "Yes, no one wants to open their lives and their home up to a stranger, to admit that they can't cope. It's tricky."

James nodded.

They sat in silence, finishing the rest of their tea.

"Have you looked at all your options, James."

James looked at her darkly, took a breath to calm himself, "yes, yes I have."

Helen smiled awkwardly and nodded, knowing not to go any further. Not this time anyway. She was not going to push things, especially after only now being reconciled with James.

James situation was different. Not unique, few things were, but his wife was young. Neither of them were ready for this and certainly weren't equipped for it. Accepting help, if indeed there was help available, was a form of giving in. At this point in their lives, this probably didn't feel like an option. They needed each other and they had each other, but sometimes that wasn't enough. Helen wished she knew what to say, she wanted to help but wasn't sure how to. Not right now anyway. She hoped that in time, James would soften and welcome her input in this respect.

"I haven't asked about you," James said out of the blue.

Helen's eyes widened, "what do you mean?"

"Well, after I had my hissy fit and stormed off, I realised that I'd been coming here and accepting your help and support but I hadn't even had the common decency to ask about you. I know bugger all about you and... well, I'm sorry. That's not like me and I'm sorry it's taken me this long to ask about you. You know, how are you? What's boiling your piss right now?"

Helen laughed, "boiling my piss, eh!?"

"Well yeah, you might be in the midst of your own crisis and here I am, swanning in and out of your life, taking, but not giving anything in return. That's totally shit, and like I say, that is not me. I'm actually a good listener. That's one of my strong points. I've dropped the ball there I'm afraid."

"So you want me to lie on the couch and tell you all my problems now?" asked Helen.

"If you wanted to, it's the least I could do," said James quite seriously.

"Well, I'm not going to do that, knowing my luck, someone would walk in and add two and two and get gross misconduct, but what about another brew and I will find something to moan about?"

"Sure," agreed James, glad at the prospect of turning the tables, and not just so he could show that he wasn't some sort of needy, emotional vampire.

"There you go," she said as she handed him his mug, filled once again with strong tea.

"Thanks," he said accepting the mug and holding it on his knee.

"I'm worried about my daughter," said Helen once she'd taken her seat.

"Drugs is it?" quipped James, instantly regretting his attempt at humour in case it really was drugs, that would put the proverbial cat amongst the pigeons and sabotage his attempt to be a proper human being, so right now he saw his chances of surviving this part of the conversation as evens at best.

"What?" Helen gave forth with a burst of laughter, "no!" she rolled her eyes, "I suppose that's something I have to be thankful for."

"What's that?" asked James.

"Well, she's very unlikely to do drugs. But part of the reason for that is currently, she's very unlikely to do much of anything," she sighed.

"Mmmm, how old is your daughter?"

"She's eighteen."
   James did a double take, "eighteen?"

"I was twelve when I fell pregnant with her," said Helen sombrely.

"Cripes! That must've been tough!" gasped James.

Helen burst out laughing, "you idiot! You crack me up! I was twenty!"

"Oh, right," James nodded, trying to look like he knew this all along, when really he'd been completely wrong footed.

"So what is your daughter..."

"Kirsty," supplied Helen.

"What is Kirsty doing now?" asked James.

"Well that's the problem, she's drifting. She's in a dead end job and she'll get sick of it and then jack it in for another dead end job and..." Helen sighed again, "she has no direction. I want something more for her, you know?"

She bit her lip and stared at James.

James met her gaze and nodded, he knew alright.

# 26

L ess than a week later, James was back at the care home. It was an unexpected visit, outside the usual weekly visit he made to Helen and the care home as she finished her shift.

In the lounge of the care home, he sat in a high backed chair. In the chair next to him was Connie. She was holding his hand and James was crying. The tears flowed down his cheeks. The terrible thing about his crying was his silence. Not a sound came from him as he sat there giving forth freely of his tears, and yet his face was contorted in the most tragic of expressions. It were as though he had been robbed of everything, including his voice.

At his feet, looking up at him despondently was Milo. The dog sat silently and patiently, not able to do anything other than to be there and to wait. He didn't look away from James. Not once.

Helen would never know how long he had been like this, only that it had been long enough. Too long. She walked into the lounge and as soon as she saw him like this she *knew*. She knew everything in that instant of seeing him in the state he was in, or at least she knew enough of it.

He didn't look up, instead he raised a hand, and in it were slightly crumpled pages to a letter. She took the proffered letter. Knew that here was the truth of it before she began to read. The letter was typed. All the better to correct it and make it make sense with the help of a laptop's software...

*Mr Dearest Jimmy-Boy,*

*If you're reading this then...*

*Then what?*

*There was a time in our lives together. A time that was not all that long ago, but now feels like a lifetime ago. In that life we had together, if you had read that opening line, then we both know what the punchline is, don't we?*

*I think I always thought that were I not to live long and prosper, I would die in the usual fashion of the beautiful young things. I would party hard and squeeze every last drop of fun and joy from life and in order to avoid ageing and any bloody hangovers, I'd drive at a hundred miles an hour at my grave and pull a handbrake turn, tyres squealing and drop unceremoniously into the earth and that would be that.*

*No! Almost forgot! There would then be the obligatory pause before the whole lot went up in a ball of flames making everyone present wonder whether I'd been take to the other place!*

*Those lives are now gone. Those people are no more. That isn't going to happen, is it? I'm not even going to get a one way trip to Switzerland am I?*

*You found The Box. My Big Secret. Or, maybe you didn't exactly find it. Who's to say? That you are aware of its existence is one of the only certainties I have left right now, in this moment of writing this letter. You know and I know you know. And yet you didn't say a thing.*

*I love you for keeping my secret.*

*I love you for always knowing the right thing to do.*

*I can trust you in a way that I never knew was possible.*

*I love you for loving me despite everything, in spite of everything.*

*It is my dearest hope that you can carry on loving me despite what it is that I have to do now.*

*That you can forgive me, and that you will in time move on and go on that date with Bjork. She needs that nearly as much as you do, and remember, she is not as tough as she makes out, she is not tough at all, so treat her as gently and respectfully as you always treated me, even when I was being an insufferable and argumentative wretch!*

*Things have been getting a lot worse recently and I can feel the end.*

*It feels like I'm in a train carriage and it's going faster and faster. I know less and less, the forgetting is horrible, it's like the forgetting makes me lighter and so I provide less and less resistance as I am dragged along.*

*So I needed to write this letter before I could no longer write it. Before a step or two eluded me so frustratingly that it was now beyond me to write it. Before I get to the stage where there is food in my mouth because I've forgotten it is there or I've forgotten to chew, possibly even forgotten how to chew!*

*I need to do something before I forget I wrote this letter, where it is, or that it even exists. How mad and bad is that? It could be the plot of one of those films you made me watch, the ones that I never could make sense of, even if I managed to stay awake until the end.*

*I'm a coward, James! I couldn't see this through and experience a death where I forgot the most basic things in my life and choked to death as I was robbed of the knowledge of how to breath. I can't imagine how horrible that would be. Not just for me. I don't want you to see me like that. I want some of who I was to remain. If I'm all gone before the end, I don't want that to be your abiding memory of me, I want you instead to remember what we had and how special it was. How lucky we both were.*

*And in case you ever do this again? Little pointer for you? Capturing past memories? Big, big tick. That saved me and gave me something to hold onto.*

*We got it wrong though! You were so intent on finding out about the rest of me, you overlooked what you already had right there in front of you. It's those memories that I treasure above all else, and the memory room was full of them. I went there frequently and it did me so much good even when I couldn't place something anymore. There was familiarity there and in our home and that grounded me.*

*Sorry, I can't help myself sometimes. You probably don't want to hear that. I just wish that we had more time, but at least we did have time. Many people don't get that. I loved the time we spent together, all of it.*

*You're one in a million, James. Don't take too long in getting back out there! Stick it to Simon and his cronies in the best way possible and don't forget to look after yourself. That includes having mindless, animalistic sex on the sofa with Kate and Katherine. At the same time if you can! Then, when you're ready, find your Bjork. But sell the sofa first and get a fresh sofa that hasn't been canoodled on.. That bit is very important, OK?*

*Telling you to move on isn't as difficult as I thought it would be. The irony is that I know you will never forget me! How sad is that!? I haven't forgotten you either my love, that is why I have to go, while I can still say that and truly mean it.*

*I love you with all my heart,*

*Melissa*

On the last sheet there were more recent handwritten words. They were written in a spidery and messy hand and Helen had to decipher not only the writing, but the correct spelling of words, their order and where they may be missing words or phrases, the meaning came through despite the difficulties the writer had experienced in putting pen to paper:

*I have to confess that I wrote that letter to you a while ago and printed it and kept it in this box for safe keeping. I took a bit of a risk in thinking that I would remember this box and what it contained. Do you want to hear a funny thing!? I was right! I remembered the box! I took it out from its hiding place and I looked down and I was shocked not to see the scan of my child, the child that I know is out there in the world somewhere, living a life I could not give him. Instead I saw these sheets of paper and I didn't know what they were. So I read them and realised that the time had come for me to say goodbye while I still could. My only sadness, my one regret, is having to say goodbye to you, but I know I must. I know that this is the right thing to do. Don't be sad for too long, OK? I'm not, I really am not. I had something that most people don't. I was happy and I had you at my side all the way. Love you, Jimmy-Boy. Be happy, if not for yourself at first, do it for me. It's the one thing I'm asking you to do. That and burn my body and scatter my ashes.*

*M X*

*PS Bugger. I don't know where my ashes were supposed to go. It's bloody robbed me of that! You'll know though. You always know what to do.*

*PPS I think I tried a video before I resorted to writing. It was awful. I should never have done that, playing it back was horrible. I remember watching myself and feeling horrible about what I was watching. I think I might also have watched it and been terribly confused. I don't think I recognised myself, let alone understood what was being said.*

*PPPS Do you remember that time that we...*
   *...no, neither do I and that is why I know it is time to go.*

Helen looked up from the pages, only now realising she was shaking with the emotion of what she had been reading.

James sensing the movement and that she had finished reading, looked up at her, his face collapsing further as he spoke through his sobbing and tears.

"I don't know where she wanted her ashes scattered! She never bloody well said!"

# 27

A *time later...*
The Red Lion stood where it had always stood, a two hundred year old building which somehow managed to remain unremarked. The place wore a cloak of semi-invisibility. A person had to stop in front of it and really focus upon it until it truly came into view. Only then did it's character and somewhat unique appearance leak through into the mind. Mostly it came to life once someone had visited and enjoyed what it had to offer, only then did it really leave its mark.

A gaunt figure walked towards the pub, huddled against the drizzling rain, barely noticeable on this grey, autumnal day. The day itself wore a cloak and beneath it's cold and wet folds nothing was worth a second look. This day was to be endured and survived. Nonetheless, this figure leaned into the weather's worst efforts, pulled his coat more tightly around him and continued along the pavement.

He was level with the door before he showed any interest in the pub at all and even then, the interest was fleeting. Then he was gone inside and the street returned to it's banality. This was possibly the most interesting thing to have happened in this locale for the past hour, not that it was noticed or noted by another living soul.

Inside, James straightened up and shrugged some of the rain from him. He opened his coat, but did not take it off.

This James was altered from the last time he had frequented these premises, his frame was leaner, slightly too lean to be healthy, and his face had taken on that gaunt and lined look that those who suffer sudden, drastic weight loss sport.

He nodded at the barman.

The barman nodded back as was the expectation in this sort of situation.

"A pint of Guinness please," said James.

Some of the warmth had absented itself from James' voice. This was not a good sign. James' warmth and humanity was what had set him apart, without that he was somehow diminished.

He drew nearer to the bar and waited for the Guinness to settle and the remainder of the pint to be poured. John was well versed in the art of barmannery and had served the Red Lion well for many a year.

James thanked him as John handed the completed pint to him. He took a drink from the pint pot and savoured the taste. This was his first visit to the Red Lion in a long time, and it appeared to have been a while since he had partaken of the black stuff too. Having savoured his return to the fold he looked around him.

As though awaiting his cue, there emerged from the far side of the pub a figure familiar to James.

Upon casting eyes upon the figure, James realised just how much he had set his hopes upon Sean being here today. There was something superstitious about this hope and James had imbued Sean with a quaint talismanic quality. His presence was enough. James superstition was a childish thing, much the same as wearing lucky socks to all his important meetings, and today he was wearing those lucky socks. They were lucky because Melissa had bought them for him before an important meeting and told him to wear them for luck. The meeting had gone well and the socks had accompanied James to all the big meetings and events in his life ever since.

He had worn those socks to Melissa's funeral.

Sean walked to the bar and smiled at James, "Aha!" he exclaimed, "the wanderer has returned!"

James, smiled. The smile took him unawares and after a flicker of surprise he gave himself to it. It felt good to smile and with it relax in company.

It had been a while.

"I take it, it went well?" asked Sean.

James almost spluttered on the mouthful of pint he was in the process of drinking.

"How?" he asked, now wearing a large and comical white moustache from his Guinness.

Sean tapped his nose, "I told you before, mate. I have *powers.*"

"He does, you know," added John the barman who was now polishing a glass as was the wont of professional bar people across the green and pleasant land on which they were now currently situated.

In the absence of a suitable reply from James, Sean persisted, "Well? Did you smash it?"

James did not reply instantly, he considered what it was that Sean may or may not know. He concluded that Sean had been in pubs long enough to read people, much the same as would-be mind-readers and future predictors did, he observed and stacked up the cues provided.

"Yes," he said eventually, "I think I did smash it."

Saying it made it real and making it real made him smile again.

"Good, I'm glad," Sean patted the top of James' arm and returned his smile, "get the man another pint on the house and I think this celebration requires additional fortification. And if

286

it doesn't, that bloody grim day out there certainly does!"

John nodded and went about his work, lifting the first of three tumblers to the whisky optic he turned his head briefly to Sean, "I take it this is a double fortification kind of a day?"

Sean nodded in business-like fashion, "of course! We don't do things by half measures here do we?"

John returned his nod. Sean was absolutely correct and not just because he was the boss, nor because he was buying.

James noted that John had included himself in this round. This was likely a long tradition and John had learnt the ropes of this particular interaction many years ago.

Drinks distributed, Sean raised his tumbler of amber liquid. He eyed the contents of the glass against what light the bar afforded, "Never ceases to amaze me and fill me with pleasure does the sight of this. There is magic and wonder here. The simple things in life should never be overlooked, nor underestimated."

No one said anything in response. This was one of those moments and it hung there awhile as they all considered life and it's simple pleasures and what they meant.

Then Sean snapped out of his reverie and returned to the business in hand, James, "to you my friend!"

They drank.

Sean raised his glass again, "to today's endeavours and your successes in them!"

They drank again.

Sean leaned on the bar, then leaned across towards James. Without realising it, James mirrored the gesture and leaned in towards Sean.

"She'd be very proud of you, you know," he said it quietly, almost too quietly to hear, but not quite.

James stifled his instinct to say pardon and ask that Sean repeat what he had said. He knew what had been said well enough. He also knew that Sean didn't know him or Melissa and so could not possibly know...

What he also wanted, was to believe in something. And this was enough. This was more than enough. Especially on the day that he had sat down with his potential backers and come to an agreement that transformed them from potential to actual backers. He now had everything in place and that included a small office, in an ideal location, just around the corner from this place.

James found that he believed a little in magic and he was intent on making magic happen. He was going to create something from nothing and improve other people's lives as a consequence. He was going to do his darndest to do things the right way. He had after all been encouraged to do so by a woman who knew him better than anyone in this world and she had believed in him totally. It was high time he went back out into the world and lived, and today was the first day of the rest of his life.

They sat there in companionable silence whilst they drank their drinks.

As he finished the last of his pint he raised his hand to catch John's attention.

"Oh no you don't!" cautioned Sean, "these are on me." He noticed John's expression as he said these words and revised them with a nod to his partner in crime, "on us."

John nodded, happy with Sean's correction, then he poured not only three fresh pints of Guinness, but three more whiskies. James had a moment of inner protest, then relaxed into the moment. This was the first time he had relaxed since...

He cast his mind back, then let that thought go. Suffice to say that it had been a while. Now was the time and he was ready for it. He smiled once more, then he leaned sideways towards Sean and spoke out of the side of his mouth, "I thought you were Mr I-Bring-Out-The-Worst-In-People?"

Sean took his whisky from John and leant back from the bar, turning so he could encompass both James and John in his reply. He opened his arms widely as though to embrace the bar itself, "Ah, now... You see... My powers are... I call myself Mr I-Bring-Out-The-Worst-In-People, because people are mostly arseholes. They can't help it, it's the way they are made. I actually shortened my full superhero name because it is *even more* cumbersome than Mr I-Bring-Out-The-Worst-In-People."

"And your full superhero name is?" James felt that he was expected to ask this question, and so he did.

He was right in this assumption, "I am glad you asked that question. It is a very good question," Sean took a swig of his whisky and gave forth of an appreciative "Ahhh! My full superhero name is, Mr I-Enhance-The-Prevailing-Quality-Or-Aspect-Of-A-Person-Which-Means-I-Bring-Out-The-Worst-In-People-Nearly-Every-Single-Bloody-Time. Man."

Sean let that sink in, "and it's worse in a pub setting. Do you know how many arseholes myself and John encounter on a daily basis?!"

"A lot," answered James.

"Yes, a lot, and the last time you visited our establishment you brought an uber-arsehole with you! What were you thinking!?"

"Yes, well, I've learnt my lesson on that score," said James.

Sean scrutinised him as though he could see whether this lesson had truly been learned by sight alone, "Yes, well of course you have, or you wouldn't be here now and in these particular circumstances. John and I certainly would not have bought you a drink if we doubted you on this score!"

Sean raised his glass and nodded knowingly at James, before tapping his own glass against his customer's, "to new friends," he toasted before drinking deeply of his Guinness and giving himself a temporary white moustache.

To new friends indeed.

James was putting his best foot forward again for the first time since Melissa's tragic death. He was back on the path and living his life. Tomorrow, he would visit another, relatively new friend and break some news to her. News related to the meeting he had had earlier today. Helen's daughter was to be James' first employee, he had spoken with Kirsty several times and they had both come to the conclusion that an apprenticeship in James' new venture would be a very good next step for her.

Just as direct and forthright as her mother, Kirsty's only reluctance in this arrangement had been that she had at first thought James was doing this out of a sense of obligation, that he was suggesting it as a favour to her Mother. James had somehow managed to miss the insinuation that his relationship with Helen was perhaps something more than friendship and he had swiftly dissuaded her of this notion of obligation, however it might have arisen. He outlined his expectations, being clear that all her hard work would pay off for her as much as it did for him. He'd seen something click with Kirsty as he talked about his vision and how she could be a part of it and from that moment he knew she would be alright and that it would be deeply rewarding for him to help her to achieve some of her potential. In turn, his talks with Kirsty enthused him and made him realise how worthwhile the venture he was embarking upon was.

He was looking forward to sharing his news with Kirsty and her Mother and only now did he realise that he was beginning to look forward again and that he still had a life ahead of him.

He still had a future.

For now though, he raised his glass in a silent toast and let himself be in the moment.

# About the Author

Jed does his very best not to take himself too seriously. There was a point in his former life where he lost his inner child, having left it in an umbrella rack in the foyer of an office near Liverpool Street Station. He is still doing his best to make amends for that unfortunate oversight and his inner child is not letting it go any time soon.

Jed Cope is the author of seven Ben and Thom books. He has also penned eight further books and a collection of short stories. He is working industriously to add to that number in the mistaken belief that he will be given a day off from writing once he's written his twentieth novel. Unfortunately, his captors got distracted by an ice cream van that had been converted into a travelling pub and completely forgot about Jed. Still, I'm sure it'll all turn out fine in the end. Usually does in circumstances such as these.

The eight books that aren't set in Ben and Thom's universes cover such genres as crime, supernatural and horror. Jed writes as he reads, across a variety of genres. Maybe he likes variety, noting that it is the spice of life, or perhaps he is hedging his bets. Whatever the case may be, he likes to write stories that have a twist or two along the way...

As well as gullible and well-meaning, Jed is a charismatic, enigmatic and pneumatic sort. Having retired from a successful career as a secret multiple F1 Champion, octopus whisperer and technology trillionaire, Jed was abducted from his underground shed where he was working on the next generation of psychic begonias, to do what he does best; make things up.

**You can connect with me on:**

🐦 https://twitter.com/jed_cope

❖ https://www.faccbook.com/jedcopeauthor

# Also by Jed Cope

So far, there are seven Ben and Thom Books:
   The Chair Who Loved Me
   Are Bunnies Electric?
   Smell My Cheese!
   Death and Taxis
   Oh Ben and Thom, Where Art Thou?
   Something Merkin This Way Comes
   Mrs Ben's Boys

Book Eight is a twinkle in the author's eye, but that twinkle is a determined wee beggar and it has a habit of making its way out into the world, so watch this space! The title may even include the word Twinkle...!

There's a children's Ben and Thom Book:
   If Only... The Adventures of an Intergalactic Chair

And seven further books that have nothing whatsoever to do with Ben and Thom:
   The Pipe
   The Entrepreneur's Club
   Two for the Show
   The Rules of Life
   Dear Kids
   Do You Remember?
   Lola's Path

And a collection of short stories:

Locked, Down and Short

Jed intends to add to the list before you've finished reading this one. It's what he does.

Printed in Great Britain
by Amazon

79853394R00173